KLABUND

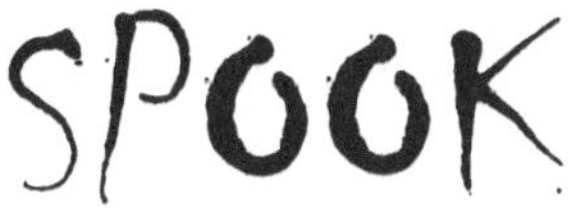

Translated by
JONAH LUBIN

THIS IS A SNUGGLY BOOK

Translation Copyright © 2023
by Jonah Lubin.
All rights reserved.

ISBN: 978-1-64525-129-3

The storm
the branch bends
the raven sings.
So wanders the weather of God
to the stars.
        —Hölderlin

SPOOK

Written during the fever of an illness.
January through April 1921.

I

THE UNDERWORLD

I had a face. The underworld rose up from my subconscious. The Acheron rushed. Charon the psychopomp landed his barge. The barge crunched on the sand. Charon leapt onto the bank. He cursed: "Here I land in hell with an empty barge. Not a single poor soul waited to cross today. Since Jesus Christ appeared for mankind, my hell and handwork lie nauseously fallow."

He rummaged around in the bag that hung on his belt.

"My bag is empty. Not a single toll. To the devil with man's virtue if I go to ruin because of it. I hate this Christ, I hate God, I hate goodness and meekness, sacrifice, truth and love."

He made the sign of hell and cried:

"O, Pluto, prince of hell, appear! Charon, the psychopomp, wishes to speak to you in deferential humility."

Thunder. The fog of the underworld parted. A bolt of lightning tore through the center of the darkness like a black satin curtain and Pluto appeared upon a fiery throne. Charon bowed: "Full of grief and bitterness I appear before your majesty. I have served you loyally and without end for thousands of years. Millions of souls over this dark stream have I led to you, that they may forever be your slaves. Upon the earth ruled your gloomy demons, your furies and spirits, and they sent soul upon soul down below. But then a miracle came to earth: God sent his only son, accompanied by hosts of silver cherubim and seraphim. They had no weapons in their hands—just staves of lilies and sunflowers—but they sent your spitting furies fleeing. God's son awakened the conscience of man. Man, so long forfeited to our dark ways, is becoming God's creation. Every day my barge carries fewer souls, and today it was completely empty. It is going poorly, Pluto—your, my, our business."

Pluto shook his serpent's head.

"I commend your zeal, servant of evil."

And his voice squealed like the shrieking of a thousand hinnys. "O you furies, you erinyes, you demons, you he-demons and she-demons, come! Pluto, your prince and sovereign, calls you!"

Amidst thunder and lightning appeared the salivating spirits and fluttering furies.

Pluto raised his scepter: a staff, cut from the tree of knowledge, and around the staff was curled a living otter with the head of a man. "Hear ye! Charon, the psychopomp, complains that day by day his barge carries fewer souls. To my displeasure I have learned that your zeal for service to the Plutonic empire has abated." He swung his scepter. "Explain yourselves, ye rebels of hell!"

A devil dared to whisper.

"The force of good is too powerful."

Pluto flared.

"Not so powerful that we might not break it. Fare ye to the overworld. Take for yourselves every shape: you a parson, you a king, you a philosopher, you a Reichstag official, you a commander, you a stockbroker, you a farmer, you a coal baron, you a barkeeper, you an old wife, you a whore. Disdain no means by which you may seduce man to every misdeed: to murder, theft, robbery, war, fornication, lies, deception, hatred, and hypocrisy.

Teach the lowest of them to turn upwards and the highest of them to turn downwards. Teach them to debase heights and exalt depths, that they may be corrupted and their souls tumble down to hell. Get you gone! You, however, lordliest of devils, Satanas, stay, for I have a special assignment for you."

The demons disappeared, hissing and howling.

But I approached Pluto's throne and bent my knee, over which the red coat, the hangman's coat, billowed, and spoke: "What do you wish, Lord of Hell, from your most devoted servant?"

Pluto spoke:

"I have been given word of a girl, sometimes called Maria, sometimes called Marianne. She is gentle and beautiful beyond compare. Her will wants good, but her youth is burdened by wishes, desires, and notions. She is wax in the hand of a decided sculptor. My spirits have told of her with such exuberance, that a great desire has befallen me to possess this soul and to call it completely my own. I intend to make her my bride. You, Satanas, will announce my courtship."

I bowed, and the red jacket rustled.

"I will forgo no seduction or temptation. Pluto will praise his most humble servant."

Pluto turned to Charon.

"And you, Charon, are you satisfied?"

Charon nodded:

"I am, Prince of Hell. My ship awaits. I am prepared."

II

THE HOUSE WITH
THE DONKEY HEADS

I was born in the house with the two donkey heads. It stands on a crooked city side street, its gable out front.

Sometimes I would stretch my head from the skylight and, if my father happened to be doing some business on the street below, he would cry out:

"Now three donkeys are sticking their heads out!"

I shrugged and laughed inaudibly.

I was neither insulted nor resentful. From a young age I felt a tender proclivity toward those grey and good-natured but spiteful equids.

Once when the dairy farmer was beating his donkey I threw myself between the latter and its torturer and felt the whip swish about my ears.

"You people should die," I screamed, "all of you should die!"

I don't know whether my parents loved me. Maybe my father. My mother hated me because she didn't want children and when I arrived I wasn't welcome. At the table she never looked at me when we spoke.

I can't recall ever receiving a glance from my mother, and to this day I don't know if she had blue or brown eyes.

I had a proclivity for space, for distance, for infinity—and a proclivity for proximity, for narrowness, for concealment.

I was a warrior and a pacifist at the same time.

When I was five years old, I walked by a toy store. There stood a small donkey on wheels. I pulled him by his string behind me, marching through the city, over the bridges, then along the causeway.

The causeway laborers called out words to me that I didn't understand.

The sun burned.

I marched, the wheels on the donkey's legs clattered.

I was picked up by a farmer who was coming into town and who recognized me from my father's shop.

He lifted me and my wooden donkey onto the wagon and brought me home.

There, I left the donkey standing by the front door, stooped to the ground, and lay down on the peat that had been swept up in a corner. It was black as night. I closed my eyes. Now only noises connected me to the world. A dog barked. A tomcat hissed. The wings of a bat rustled. The sound of the mortar my father was pounding emerged from the court-yard. Wagons rolled. Adults cried nonsensical sounds to each other. Children no older than myself laughed and cried.

I lay outside of this world, completely by myself.

Only the two donkey heads and the wooden donkey abandoned on the street, my worldly proconsul, were the confidants of my mute secrets.

But they knew how to keep quiet—like me.

III

THE BLOOD BROTHERHOOD

WHO was my friend?

The donkey from the dairy farm or the dusty chestnut tree in the courtyard that looked as if it had waited in the ware-yard for a long time because a customer had placed an order for it but not picked it up.

Who was my girlfriend?

Some cloud or glistening gnat or a white wave in the choppy stream.

My first encounter with a person my age went like this: for my birthday I was given a sailor suit and a sailor hat. I went around in this uniform, a little barge carved from bark upon my arms, over the meadow to what they called Gänselache. There I sat myself down in the grass and let the barge float. It was not long before a boy my age, but totally unkempt and infected with lice, with an evil look in his cat eyes, was standing next to me. He splashed his naked feet in the water. His eyes streaked over my uniform.

"Give me your cap," he said out of nowhere.

I didn't know how to respond and stayed silent.

Just like an adult the boy pulled a knife from his back pocket and turned on me.

I was so frightened that I let slip the tow rope and the bark barge, which I had carved with such effort, whirled away down an eddy.

I already felt the knife in my neck when I heard the voice of an adult. I must admit that, although in that moment I was in mortal danger, I perceived it with extreme annoyance. Adults have an insufferable habit of interfering high-handedly in the activities and commerce of children, which firstly do not concern them and secondly they do not understand.

I looked up and saw Leidl the cobbler, a disreputable person, grabbbing the knife from the ragged boy and throwing it into the river. The boy bit his hand till it bled, but the cobbler only smiled and spoke the words that he always said and that the street urchins would call after him: "Don't be bad!"

Then he smiled the first smile I'd ever seen on a human face and spoke:

"Is it the boy's fault that his father has money and yours doesn't?"

And he spoke to me:

"You have done the boy an injustice without knowing it. Give him your hand." I gaped in surprise and didn't understand a single thing the cobbler was saying. The boy had come at me with a knife and it was I who had done him an injustice?

But gnawed by doubt I gave the boy my hand which he took with resistance.

"Now play together!" said the cobbler and left.

So we sat together on the sandy bank.

I looked at him and he lowered his head.

He looked at me and I lowered my head.

Suddenly a thought came to me. I took the cap from my head and said:

"The cap's yours now. I'm giving it to you."

He seemed to doubt my sincerity.

"And what if you're lying? Everybody lies."

"You can have my sailor's cap. I really don't like it."

He grimaced and behind it there was a bitter taste in his mouth.

"Oh, so since you don't like it that means it's good for me?"

"No, no," I was ashamed. "I really like it—I got it for my birthday today."

Then the boy took it, put it on, and said:

"My name is Munk and I'm the son of Munk the butcher."

I said my name to him, but left out the name of my father who was not in the same league as a butcher and slaughterer in terms of importance and raw power, although he earned more money.

"We need to swear blood brotherhood," said Munk. "Damn," he rumpled his forehead like an adult, "but this pig—now *he* should be slaughtered—but this Leidl the Cobbler threw my knife in the river. "*Don't be bad, don't be bad,*" he mimicked the cobbler. "Only be bad! Only be bad!" he erupted. "Do what my dad does to animals to people. For sure. And here comes this cobbler who drank away his business and beat his wife to death and he's concerned with our social mores."

He said: "social mores". God knows where he had picked that up. He went searching on the bank.

Reeds stuck out of the shallow beach water. He bent a stalk over towards himself and snapped it with great expertise to produce a point. With this he began to bore a little hole in his upper arm until he drew blood.

"Now drink!" He said.

And I drank his blood.

It had a stale, cloying taste.

If only I hadn't drunk it!

Then he inflicted a small wound on me and drank my blood. "Now we're bound forever, we're blood brothers," said Munk, giving me a strange sidelong glance. "Visit me sometime on slaughtering day."

IV

THE SATURNIA MOTH

IT'S midday, 11:30. I sit at my table. I only have one table: I use it to work, to play, to eat. The little yellow lamp burns: my room looks out onto the courtyard—here day never breaks. For weeks the garbage in the court-yard hasn't been taken away. The garbagemen are striking. I barely need to open the window and a yellow, simum-like, evil-smelling cloud wafts into my room. I got up very early today. Usually I stay in bed till two, three, yes some-times till 4 p.m.

That is: I don't own a bed. The room has no place for that. It's a sort of daybed.

It's cold in the room. Outside the eastern wind whistles. The lamp's yellow light does me good. It reminds me of my room way down south, where one didn't freeze and where the

22

same yellow lampshade hung around the lamp. Maria herself cut it out of a scrap of silk. Since then I've disdained the sun and this yellow light is all I need.

Till now I've had my eyes closed. Now I open them and, somewhat surprised, find myself back in the world again. An engraving on the wall: *Love's Spring.* A petty-cash cavalier in a Roman tunic leaning over an Etruscan barmaid. A bookcase with a glass door behind which book titles are legible. The case is always closed. Since the books belong to my landlord.

The room smells a little like aromatic vinegar; I rub myself with it early in the morning since at night I have a tendency to sweat.

The doorbell rang earlier and I have a feeling that some sort of telegram or express letter is on the table in the corridor. I had forbidden the girl to disturb me. Should I take a look? It doesn't really matter. Sometimes I don't open telegrams for four weeks. Perhaps the house with the donkey heads has collapsed or a fiery catastrophe has razed it to the ground. It's all the same to me. That wasn't meant to be nonchalant. Rather: it's—all—the—same, I am my destiny, and this telegram will bring me as little out of my equilibrium as the death of a loved one or my own death would. I have gone beyond my death and beyond myself. I have suffered too much. It is all only here to attest to me: the eastern wind, the aromatic vinegar, the yellow lamp, the beloved woman, death.

When I began to love Maria, I knew from the very first day with a painful, bittersweet certainty that I would kill her: without intent, without awareness of a goal or a purpose. Just as Munk had wanted to kill me when he came at me with a knife because I was embarrassed to give him an answer.

Destiny asked a question of me and I killed Maria——because I was embarrassed to answer. I defended myself with all my spiritual power against the morbid desires I felt for her even in the loveliest moments of fulfillment and perfection. As if it happened yesterday I remember that summer's night on the Silbersee. A stupefying, beautiful scent of flowers and stars lay in the air. The flowers shone. The stars smelled. The summer crickets still chirp in my ears. We lay on the veranda, swathed only in the violet blue twilight. I felt Maria's smile viscerally: "I'm so happy, that this happiness cannot last." I turned my head.

I'd been touched by the cascading wing of a saturnia moth.

V

THE STONE GUEST

I put on my coat and went out onto the street. The first snow had covered the pavement with a thin white glaze. The angels in heaven plucked wool bandages. There were so many wounds to bind: both here and beyond. At Hallesches Tor I bought a newspaper from a newspaper woman who was known as Tomato because of her red facial rash. The newest political happenings did not interest me, I only thumbed through the classifieds in the back, looking for death announcements to see if anybody whose name I bore had died. I'm wildly superstitious. The day began with an ill omen. Indeed: someone had died. The director of a joint stock company. Five obituaries were printed: from the family, the board of directors, the office staff, the workers. Five times

25

I read my name surrounded by a black border. I took my hat off. Tomato grumbled: "You'll catch a cold, mister. It's snowing." I turned onto Belle-Alliance-Strasse. The cemetery lay in the middle of the city, like a medieval fortress surrounded by a red wall. Even in death the people were barracked in. As in life as in death, only the ostracized, the criminals, the murderers and the Jews have their place outside the walls. I tried the rusted cemetery gate, which creaked at the hinges like a dancer past her prime. I walked along the main path. The snow decked all the graves with delicate, white lace cloths. You are envied! You are blessed! You rest! I tumble, fever, burn as always. You are heavenly cool! Paradisacally silent! I feel a noose around my neck, a snake around my neck like a dervish. The noose thrown over the horn of the moon—and the earth viewed from high above must seem deep below.

I felt a shadow come up behind me. The cemetery free of people.

"Who are you?" I cried.

"Neither friend nor foe" intoned the answer.

I dared to look around.

"You are pursuing me."

"You've dragged me here."

I left the main alley and stepped into a side path that led to the wall. There on the wall lay a grave that I loved and feared, that for some months I had not been visiting. A white marble plaque displayed the name: "Maria" and nothing else.

I sat myself down on the grave's enclosure.

Snow fell onto the earth, through the earth and onto the coffin, through the coffin and onto the heart. Snow fell onto the heart.

The shadow stood threateningly behind me.

Over on the street, above the red wall, a window was open. A piano teacher taught her pupil the overture to *Don Giovanni*.

"Here lies Donna Anna, Donna Maria interred," said the shadow. I sensed icy breath on the back of my neck. "You brought her under the earth. Beware: the stone guest invites you to the funeral banquet."

I glanced up.

A stone statue of Roland stood next to me above a soldier's grave. The stone knight examined me with hostility. Then he moved his eyelashes. I heard his armor clatter. His eyes squinted severely against the snow's light. Then, with effort, he lifted his legs and climbed down from his pedestal. He swaggered over to me with his sword raised in both hands. Screaming, I jumped up and fled towards the exit. I paused at the portal.

The clanging of a passing trolley calmed me down. How ridiculous I was. That I no longer had my nerves under control. I had become feverish. That was probably why I saw ghosts in broad daylight.

I looked warily around me.

The stone guest had followed me.

My heart stood still. I could no longer avoid him. He stepped toward me:

"Can I have a light?"

It was the cemetery watchman, a short pipe in the corner of his mouth. He wore a white sheepskin.

VI

THE TRANSPARENT LADY

THAT same evening at around 10 p.m. in the Green Paintbrush cabaret I suffered the hemorrhage that the press had correctly reported—though, if I might add, not very tastefully. Kontack the Comic, a man with a head of bone but a heart of gold, had just sung a recently popular crime ballad for an auditorium full of criminals who gestured apoplectically and roared hoarsely along with the refrain. Then it happened.

I was in the audience. No one recognized me. I had lain my hands on my forehead and felt my blood pounding: then I saw two eyes pointed towards me that I knew had been searching for me for a long time. Well, at first I didn't see them, but I sensed that there were two eyes in the hall that wanted to look into my own. When you look over, I said to myself, something will happen. The roof will collapse. The plague will break out in Berlin. Europe will perish. You'll have a heart attack. Or you'll be forced to exhibit yourself before these eyes, before this audience. Something horrifying, unimaginable will happen. Because these eyes are the only eyes before which I cannot be in front of. My entire life is in them. My guilt. My desire. My doubt, my love, my crime.

These eyes are her eyes.

I shuddered at the thought: that she's really dead—but her eyes must still be alive, since these eyes were sharply, brightly, and clearly directed towards me.

Eyes by themselves, I contemplated in contradiction, are incapable of life. Eyes do not hover in the air like butterflies, though these eyes do have something moth-like about them. Eyes, if they are to see, must sit in a person's head, must be connected with sinews and the optic tract to the brain. Eyes are not there in-and-of-themselves.

This contemplation gave me the courage to turn and look into her eyes—and I had to laugh at my fear and trepidation. The eyes I looked into smiled at me with tenderness and love. They belonged to a young lady of about eighteen years who sat a couple of tables away from me with a gentleman whose face I could not discern, covered by the broad backs of fat leather dealers or coarse butter profiteers. Then I heard her half-whisper to her partner with a quick glance towards me: "That's him." Drops of sweat appeared on my forehead.

What was the significance of this utterance?

What did this lady, who was completely unfamiliar to me, know that let her dare say it—was she a detective? The detective squad was supposed to have recently modernized: perhaps the blonde young lady was a detective.

Then the audience began to clap. The lady clapped heartily too, letting glances fall softly upon me, and then I knew what she had meant with her mysterious utterance—I was already so extremely nervous that I sought double meanings in even the simplest, clearest occurrences. Kontack had just sung a couplet of mine, and that the lady perhaps knew me from the cabaret (since I sometimes used to perform my own couplets) would not have been so shocking. There were certainly other people who knew me in the hall. That is, who knew me quite superficially. No one had even the slightest idea or intimation of my true, real life. At the thought that no one knew me, I had to laugh out loud, which outraged some of the guests and induced them to hiss "pst!"

at me. I smothered my laughter with a smile which I sent over to that blonde lady and lifted my wine glass in a secret toast to her.

She noticed the greeting and returned it slightly. A pleasant adventure, I thought to myself. So completely to my taste. She is young, lithe, blonde, and since she knows who I am, she will fly to me. There'll be no difficulties or disputes. That's not for me. All that was left to consider was how to tear her away from that man at the table.

Suddenly she stood up.

Ah! an encouraging sign. Beautiful—this is shaping up nicely. She threw me a glance from the sapphire blue eyes behind her long lashes and walked—she had been sitting at the table to the right of the stage—elevated by the stage's bright lights, past the stage, and out of the crepuscular viewing room.

And then it happened.

She had the light at her back.

After I had seen her profile for a few steps, she turned to face me.

And I saw, the blood curdling and freezing in my veins, that the lady was completely transparent. I saw through her clothes and her flesh and I saw nothing but a skeleton and a skull, and in the skull her eyes burned.

I had stood up with the intent to follow her, but then suddenly I felt the stiff curdled blood in my veins liquefy, a stream of fire began to rush through me, and in an instant my mouth was full of hot blood that had sprung from the depths of my body, as if I were a volcano, and then the stream of blood broke out over my lips and I fell lengthwise in the middle of the cabaret like a board to the floor.

VII

THE BLEEDING HEART

WHEN I awoke I found myself in a speeding car. Are they filming some sort of movie and maybe the car's not really moving and maybe two men are just shaking it back and forth to evoke the illusion of movement?

I bent forward a little.

I saw the chauffeur through the glass. Saw houses and trees and people and trolley stops race by.

The car was really moving.

I leaned back in the upholstery—then I felt a hand on the back of my head.

I turned to the side:

A lady who was completely unfamiliar to me was sitting with me in the car. I wanted to speak, but she laid her finger on my lips, indicating that I should be quiet.

And then, all of a sudden, I sensed a stale, cloying taste in my mouth—as I did when I drank with Munk to our blood-brother-hood—and I came to myself and remembered: I had suffered a hemorrhage in the cabaret—but what had happened before?

That I could not remember.

I closed my eyes. I opened them again and noticed the presence of a third person in the car: a gentleman, whose features I was unable to decipher because he sat in the lady's shadow.

I was reminded of her presence by the gentle pressure of her hand. I reciprocated that pressure gently. "Who are you, who is looking after me so lovingly?"

The woman laid her fingers on my lips:

"Do not speak! You need to recover. And it is none of your concern who loves you."

And the voice of the man emerged from the darkness:

"Hyacinthe, tell the gentleman that he should be quiet. If he talks he will suffer another hemorrhage."

I spoke no further because this voice had a tone that almost forced you to silence. And yet it sounded neither comfortable nor awkward, neither good nor evil, neither beautiful nor ugly, but completely extraneous.

I looked out the window.

The car drove through the zoo.

Snow lay on the lawns and icicles hung from the trees.

Snow tempers pain, I thought, and didn't know why I thought it.

Snow falls onto the heart like earth onto the coffin and like tears onto the deathbed.

I racked my brains.

Tears must once have flowed on the deathbed.

Earth must once have fallen onto the coffin. Snow must once have fluttered onto the heart.

Rose-colored veils constricted before my eyes. Red spiders sat at the intersections where the threads were knotted. Everything I saw was divided into red diamonds, like country sheets, like a chessboard. Queen's check, I thought.

I couldn't think any further. I was far too dazed from the hemorrhage.

But when I turned to the lady at my side, my eyes widened in disgust.

I saw nothing but her black silhouette and in this black silhouette a red, twitching heart.

And this heart—bled.

Snow fell outside behind the car window and seemed to fall into the bleeding heart, where the white snowflakes transformed into blood-red tears.

Was someone crying for me?

"It's not true!" I cried. "Her heart no longer lives! it can no longer live! because I buried it one winter's night in the snow—"

The heart burned like a red light in the black car.

The snow fell: onto the world, onto the wagon, onto me.

> Black is the night,
> and red is the heart,
> and white, so white is the snow—
> The snow went up to my neck, then I
> fell into a faint.

VII

CHARITÉ

I awoke with a jolt.

The car had stopped.

"Charité!" cried the chauffeur.

"I'll take him under his left arm, you take him under his right," said the lady.

I was so weakened that I had to look in front of me in order to put one leg in front of the other. Who's walking? I absolutely don't want to walk at all. It is walking.

"Chauffeur, please wait longer!" said the voice, which was neither good nor evil.

I lay down on the leather sofa in the receiving room.

An assistant doctor with an English pipe hanging crookedly from his mouth approached me in a state of discontent.

"Seeing as it's 11:55, and therefore is technically still today, you will be billed for today as well. Do you understand?

I understood and moved my head weakly.

Everybody's hustling today. Everybody wants to do business. He'll probably tuck the money for today in his pocket. He's probably poorly paid. Charité—what does that mean in German? It seems like some sort of medical grift in any case. Tubercular waiters for neighbors. Fast and loose with the ethics. There's only one spiro-ethic in these spermatazoa.

"You have to pay!" cried the assistant doctor and in his rage the pipe nearly fell out of his false teeth.

An attendant with the head of a warthog who had since shuffled in nodded with Schadenfreude.

"You must pay eight days in advance, and then you can be admitted..."

Mercy! What kind of people are these!

And then I knew what Charité meant:

Mercy...

I fumbled in my breast pocket to take out my wallet and calm the repulsive condemner.

The wallet was gone!

Agitated, I sat up.

I looked through all my pockets.

Nothing to find.

The wallet was gone.

"But I still had my wallet in the cabaret!"

"He who has, has," said the warthog, "and he who had, had.""But—"

"But, but," the assistant doctor mocked, "did you know the gentleman and the lady who dropped you off here?

Which gentleman—and which lady—oh—I remember—I looked around—they were no longer there.

"No, I did not know the gentleman and the lady who were kind enough to stand by me in my time of misfortune... How long has it been since they left... weren't they just here?

"They just left a couple of minutes ago—and," the attendant and the assistant doctor yelled with pleasure, "they were probably kind enough to attend to your wallet..."

"What does that mean?" It was difficult to comprehend in my state of weakness.

"That you likely fell into the hands of crooks and that somebody has stolen your wallet from you."

"Pinched," said the attendant with the warty head, "lifted, nabbed, pilfered."

"That's impossible!" I protested as best I could, "the lady belonged to highest circles of society."

The attendant approached the leather sofa.

"If you can't pay, we can't keep you here."

I raised myself weakly.

"But I can barely walk…"

Then I saw the attendant in front of me:

He had a knife in his hand and his white apron was splattered with blood.

"Butcher!" I cried and jumped to my feet.

"Butcher!" the walls echoed back.

I stumbled past the concierge.

The door snapped shut behind me.

Free! free again! not imprisoned! The image of the blood-splattered butcher, who looked like Munk's father when he came from the slaughter, disappeared.

I rested my hot head on the cool wall.

I breathed out deeply.

But this deep breath tore my breast.

A fresh stream of blood sprang forth and, sinking to my knees, I colored the snow with my blood.

Snow didn't fall onto the bleeding heart—

Blood dripped onto the white snow.

IX

THE MAN WITH THE HANDCART

A man with a handcart trotted past.

When he saw me kneeling in the snow with my hands plunged forward—from afar I must have looked like a dog—he stopped.

"What's this? You been drinking? You've had a little too much infant spirits? Or have you lost six pence in the snow?"

Then he noticed the flecks of blood in the snow.

He shook his head.

"Oh good God—what sort of hard-hearted people these days. Here they're letting a poor consumptive croak in the snow just like that." He took me under my arm, hoisted me high and dumped me onto his hand cart.

He covered me with an old overcoat that was lying on the cart and found a cardboard

42

box for my pillow. It clattered and rattled as he shoved it under my head.

"Where do you live?"

I gave him my address.

"That's right in my neighborhood—here, hold this sack so it doesn't roll off."

And he shoved a rather heavy canvas sack beside me on the cart.

As I took it in my arms like a child I sensed an ice-cold human hand through the canvas.

And this hand was delicate and narrow like her hand.

After the experiences of that evening I was no longer capable of an excess of emotions like pain, horror, disgust, and fear.

I lay there quiet and stiff.

An icy wind blew over my forehead: in lightning quick, sharp bursts.

It was as if I was in a duel, without a weapon, defenseless, and every couple of seconds my opponent's sharp, pointed blows cut into my cheeks and forehead.

But blood didn't flow. It seemed to freeze immediately in the terrible cold.

Who was my opponent? Who strove relentlessly toward my annihilation?

God! God!

I was sent forth by the Devil as a sparkling frigate and came ashore to God as an unrigged wreck.

The man pushed the cart.

The wind abated.

The clouds dissolved in the air. More and more stars emerged. In golden facets they ordered themselves symmetrically into the eye of a gigantic fly that stared down at me.

The man stopped at Reichstagufer.

He listened to the night.

The fly's eye had disappeared. The stars glistened like flowering frost on the sky's window: behind that, music rang out, barely perceptible, like grasshoppers chirping from a great distance.

The Spree flowed quietly.

Drowsy and shivering, the houses pressed up onto one another.

The man yanked the sack from the wagon and dragged it over the bridge's landing.

A dull, blunt splash in the babbling water. He listened for another moment.

"Alright then!"

He rubbed his hands, which were blue from frost, and shoved the cart further down the trolley tracks.

"Are you a criminal?"

I asked this quietly, no longer capable of revolt, excitement, or indignation.

He spoke to the air in front of him as if he were talking to himself:

"Here lies the old woman in her shroud, in repose on her chaise longue. It had snowed all day but it is evening now and the sun storms and plunges through the opened window with a golden shout. A young woman, my bride, stands in front of the mirror and combs her long hair, tears in her eyelashes. The old woman has snow-white hair. It has snowed all day. Her whole life long. Her body is that of a young woman: delicate, lithe, with an astonishing complexion. The girl at the window turns occasionally to the dead woman and every time her glance falls upon her face or breast, she smiles or curls her lips with pain or a little anger. I too will lie like that someday, having died some other way, but death is death, she thinks: in a few decades—or years—or months? Who knows? Tomorrow there's a dance in the tents and I'll go dancing.

"I sit at the bed and think about everyone I've seen die, and that dying is bitter, but that death, when the limbs have relaxed after hours of agony, must be sweet. Like how your limbs collapse when you've finally fallen asleep.

"The girl at the mirror tests her hairdo.

"Then she turns to me and says:

"'Come, we must go.'

"Her voice dies away out of fear.

"I press her hand very firmly and realize that I have no pity for the dead woman. There are pains that preclude the possibility of their worsening and that force one to regard the pain that others can feel as negligible. It has been two years since my beloved died and left me, and what died then was youth, happiness, future. Here on the ottoman lies an old woman who fulfilled her purpose and who will be remembered as: the good old woman... But before they said: the beautiful, young woman... What died then, died under the sidereal sign. The genius extinguished his torch in the earth. The sun went out.—A breeze wafts through the window.

"Some snowflakes fall upon the snow-white hair of the dead old woman.

"The girl steps away from the mirror.

"She steps up to the bed and, with a slight shudder, kisses the dead woman on the forehead and kisses me, still alive, on the lips."

He went silent and shoved the cart.

The cart crunched through the snow.

I opened my eyes which I'd held closed for the duration of the story.

"Aren't you worried that I'll turn you in?"

The man shook his head.

"When you were lying in the snow—in your blood—I sensed that you were a comrade of mine. I saw your eyes for a moment in the shine of the gas lamps."

"And—?"

"You have a left eye that one does not forget after he has looked into it. And this left eye—it's the eye above the heart—betrays who you are to he who can see."

I smiled weakly.

"And what did you see in my left eye?"

"The likeness of a murdered woman hangs in your pupil..."

I made no attempt to dispute this adventurous and fantastic claim.

Indeed, could I dispute it at all?

I was silent.

The cart creaked.

The stars began to ring like tiny silver bells.

"Who was that who you threw over the bridge?"

He turned his head in a spiral like a ruminating parrot.

"A good old woman. Seventy-nine years old. She lived at Krausnickstrasse 23. We waited in her apartment until she returned home. Then I stuffed an ether-soaked handkerchief in her mouth. She owned a small corner jewelry store. There's some trinkets that interested me in the cardboard box you're lying on: a leather bag made of black human skin, a chain made of the bones of Javanese children with platinum fastenings, and a golden necklace whose links are real, glazed human eyes."

X

THE HOUSE OF PAIN

I'D made it to my apartment.

I climbed from the cart and shook the man's hand for taking me so far with him.

"Unfortunately, I have nothing to give you. My wallet's gone astray."

"Oh," he commiserated with a lively gesture "we black brothers should, at the very least, do no harm to each other. It's not fair to steal from a thief or to murder a murderer. Such things should be reserved for bourgeois society, which of course cracks at every joint regardless. Either way all my needs are quite well provided for."

He pulled out a wallet.

"How much can I help you out with, comrade?"

He plucked a hundred mark note and pressed it into my hand, which closed, baffled, and he disappeared around the corner with his cart.

Like an echo, his voice rang again and again in my ears. Upon the final repetition I recognized this voice. I hadn't heard it for many years.

There was no doubt that the man with the cart had been Munk. I walked or staggered until I reached my door and pulled out my house key.

I stuck it in the lock.

It didn't fit.

I tried once again.

What the hell? Did somebody go and change the lock in the middle of the night?

I looked at the key. There was no doubt: it was my house key.

Then I apprehended a voice coming from inside the house.

"Come in. Now, doll. Do come in. Come tickle my little head."

It was the voice that I had sworn never to hear again. The voice that had accompanied the horrible events of my life with its hollow, senseless chattering.

I stumbled a couple of steps back and looked at the house number. Without realizing it, I had given the man with the handcart the address of my former apartment. It was the house of pain, the house where I had lived with her.

"Tickle my little head... Maria," the parrot squawked. I turned and ran with superhuman strength, stumbled, crept the half hour to my current residence. I constantly feared that someone was behind me: the police, the parrot, the man with the cart, the man from the car, the attendant with the blood splattered apron from Charité, Kontack the Comic, Pluto with his serpent head and otter scepter. I threw myself into my narrow little room that opened up onto the courtyard and in which it never became day, and, still dressed, onto the daybed after having hastily barred and locked the door.

And I fell into a deep and heavy sleep.

XI

THE PICTURE

WHEN I awoke, the yellow lamp on the table was burning. I had forgotten to turn it off the previous evening.

The yellow light did me good.

Outside was a grey and gloomy day. The light of day seeped only sparingly through the curtains of the single-window room. It reeked of aromatic vinegar.

I looked at the clock: 11:30 a.m.

I sighed deeply, as if released.

I was home alone.

The bluish moonstone twinkled on the clock, and the little Indian cat made of yellow marble stood next to it. And below the lamp: suffused with the pale holy light of the lamp-shade: her picture.

Her hand held the white rose before her at her breast as if for protection. Her blonde hair was pinned up high. Her lips, half open, revealed her delicate teeth. But her eyes—her goodly eyes looked at me with anger.

What did that mean?

Wasn't it true she'd forgiven me?

Had her forgiveness been a travesty?

Had she only superficially forgiven me in order now to martyr me all the more horribly: like in the time of the inquisition when the imprisoned would be allowed to run away through innumerable halls and dozens of gates—and just when they'd passed the final one and made it onto the open field and the feeling of final freedom began darkly to intoxicate them: the hangman would suddenly spring from the soil before them, red like a gigantic poppy? Fragments of memory from the events of the previous night flew across my consciousness like clouds in the wind.

And I remembered: that yesterday her eyes had sought mine; that her eyes, the eyes of a dead woman, still lived in this world, on this earth.... They compelled me to look into them, to reflect myself in them—and wanted to draw me to reckoning.

Why didn't I ask the man who'd stolen the bracelet with the human eyes to show it to me? Wasn't it possible that her eyes were among them? Why didn't I take down this man's address?

I should have bought the bracelet from him... madness... this was of course madness... murderers don't present their calling card to just anyone.

Once more I looked over to the picture.

Her eyes shone like two moonstones.

The moonstone that she'd left me as a talisman had been her secret symbol.

I looked into her eyes.

They had safeguarded me loyally.

I saw myself.

Everywhere was me——me——me.

Oh how I hated myself, how eager I was to extinguish myself from human memory, theirs and mine.

I groped for the picture.

Her lips seemed to move and it seemed to me she spoke those words that Leidl the Carpenter had always spoken:

"Don't be bad."

I opened the frame, took the photograph out and cut her eyes from her head with the little scissors that lay on the table.

XII

THE LETTER

THERE was a knock.

I started and hid the picture in my bed.

"Who's there?"

It was the maid, Elise.

I went to the door and opened it.

She brought breakfast and the post.

I crept immediately back into the cushions.

I was unspeakably miserable.

I felt my pulse. There was no doubt I had a fever. The most reasonable thing to do would be to stay in bed. Last night's damned hemorrhage. How do you bear it?

Among the letters were business inquiries, among them one proposing I put in a guest appearance at the Fledermaus cabaret in Koenigsburg for 8,000 marks a month. That engagement has also gone to hell by now, and I could have really used that 8,000 marks, by God, I don't even have a decent suit anymore.

Another letter: a teacher from Schmachtenhagen, Kreis Krossen, requested an autograph from me. The Lessing Society in Braunschweig, the Observatory in Mannheim, the literary society in Nuernberg, and the bookstore Esplanade in Hamburg inquired as to whether I would like to come to them and read "from my works." From my works. These couplets I produce they call works. I feel ill. If this society and these societies only knew what all my work is, out of which I won't read because I myself cannot decipher it.

I write hieroglyphs.

Eventually I found another private letter.

"To Herr .....t"

From a girl, probably, judging by the orthography. I opened it:

Berlin, ... Hospital
Ward 2, Room 20
You are hereby notified that Miss Marianne has been admitted to the hospital. Miss Marianne would have written herself, but she is suffering from a high fever. Visiting hours: Wednesday, Saturday, and Sunday 2-3.
Best regards, for Miss Marianne

The signature was illegible.

Again a pink veil began to pass before my eyes. I wracked my brain in vain trying to figure out how I could have come upon this letter and who this Miss Marianne was supposed to be. I had loved many women, perhaps Miss Marianne was one of them. Perhaps she remembers me because it's going poorly for her now. Naturally, I would send her 50 marks. God knows you can't get back on your feet with 50 marks these days but at the very least she'll see my good will.

Then, as fast as lightning, an idea flashed through my mind: ward 2, that's the maternity ward. This suspicion didn't deceive me, no chance.

I, myself a spawn of hell, demonically sealed and consecrated by Pluto the Prince of Hell himself, had again brought a child into the world, a miserable child into this godforsaken world, into this festering abscess of a (perhaps-soon-to-come) true world.

But who was the mother?

Marianne... Marianne... I repeated this name three times, completely senselessly, and it did not become more familiar. I had lived the last half year like never before in my life.

Because I wanted to free myself from her.

And yesterday's hemorrhage was certainly the result of these insane ramblings: because, not satisfied with a single woman, some days I embraced two or three. In the car. On the floor. At the zoo. I rarely took the trouble to bring them back home with me. It was impossible to rememember their names or even their features. A few weeks ago at a party I made the acquaintance of a lady who, once we had retreated to a corner of the Wintergarten, showed a familiarity for me that both attracted and estranged me. Only after a while did I realize, that is recall: I had once spent the night with this lady but completely forgotten.

Who was the young mother in the hospital?

Contortionists, actresses, young ladies of so-called society, maids, flatterers, chansonettes, fifteen-year-old girls, married women and mothers marched before me in a long row: who was it?

Their shapes were shadowy, their faces—ambiguous, I had forgotten their names, but occasionally a name shot up like: Lotte, Lilly, Anny, Grete—I only knew one thing: that I had loved them all, not as one loves dolls or glass beads, but as one loves stars and animals and flowers.

XIII

THE ALBINO

THE doorbell rang.

I jolted up.

The police?

I heard the maid in the corridor negotiating: "But he is still lying in bed..."

A voice whose harmonious tones enchanted me responded. "Oh, that doesn't matter—please just let us in."

There was a knock and then they entered: the lady and gentleman from yesterday evening.

The woman wore a seal skin and a small black hat. Judging by her features (which she concealed beneath a finely meshed veil, a dragonfly pinned to her left cheek) she was barely 20. She held a bouquet of lilacs in her hand, which, with a smile, she set down onto the cushions.

The gentleman behind her had materialized properly in a top hat which he subsequently discarded. He undid his mink and an old-fashioned frock coat came into view.

Then he approached me. I saw for the first time his face, his eyes.

He was an albino.

His eyes were red like those rabbits. He wore a fringed beard like Leidl the Cobbler.

His head and facial hair were snow-white, though by my estimate he was at most forty years old.

"We called Charité. You were no longer there. So, how's it going? Please do not speak loudly—you should only speak softly—your lungs must heal and remain as still as possible—stay lying on your back—I will percuss and auscultate—so well as I can without straining you."

He pulled back the covers.

The lilacs fell to the ground.

The lady picked them up nonchalantly and stuck them in the carafe of water on the washbasin.

The albino knocked on my chest and I don't know why I put up with his manipulations. Who had sent for the doctor?

"On the right, acute dullness—that seems to be an old spot—have you had a cavity? The hemorrhage must have begun there."

He fumbled in his breast pocket and pulled out a collapsible stethoscope. He screwed it together and placed it on my breast:

"Breathe normally—do not strain yourself—please whisper: ninety-nine—again—ninety-nine—ninety-nine—"

I sat up.

"You can no longer remain in this cramped, dark room without sufficient light or air. You must go to a sanatorium or hospital—do not interrupt me—you need rest, care, and a nurse"—with that his glance fell upon the blonde lady—"should attend to you around the clock. I have already brought the ambulance. It is waiting in front of the door."

I didn't know what I should say.

The red eye pierced through me.

The lady walked up to the bed and took my hand.

"You have to do something to help yourself. I cannot in good conscience leave you here so helpless and deserted."

But, as I felt her hand, which lay icy cold in my feverish hand like that of a corpse, it came over me again: "Leave me—leave me alone—you don't know who you are offering your help to—to whom you give your good and beautiful hand. Don't bend yourself too near to me or you'll meet the miasma of my breath. Don't look me in the eye. Don't look me in my eye. Don't look into my left eye, the eye above my heart. Dread dwells in my eyes. A handshake from me is as poisonous as the sting of a scorpion."

The red-eyed man stood there, his hands crossed behind his back.

"T.B. with a psychogenetic cause. This requires a sputum analysis, of course, but first and foremost an analysis of the entire soul."

The lady leaned over me such that I could sense her breath, and it smelled sweet like oleander or almonds or hyacinths. "My dear man, please do not be anxious, please do not be afraid. Even if you were a criminal or a murderer, I would still care for you. I would neither love you less nor be any less good to you. What do I care who and what you are? I have no right to ask about that, only the duty to help you."

I had half sat up in the cushions.

My heart raced in bliss.

If salvation was possible, it was only possible because I loved this woman.

The albino fumbled again in his frock coat.

"By the way, here is your wallet. You left it in the car yesterday."

The door sprang open.

Two orderlies entered with a stretcher. Behind them was the maid Elise with tears in her eyes, wringing her hands.

I was laid on the stretcher.

The red eye fascinated me. I did not dare revolt and suddenly felt deathly weak.

I was carried through the hallway.

Curious residents, old women, a girl in a Scottish blouse, a lame customs inspector, some children were already waiting.

The customs inspector lifted his cane, lending him the appearance of Kaiser Friederich the Great, and crowed:

"That's what he gets for his carrying on like that! Now he's consumptive."

Shuddering, the women huddled in their headscarves and shawls. The young girl smiled sheepishly, helplessly. The children looked at me with open mouths and one said: "Look, he's dead! Come on, let's go play at being dead."

XIV

THE FANTASTIC FOREST

HYACINTH held my hand the whole way.

The ambulance had frosted windows so that you couldn't see where it was going. And it also smelled like creosote, lysoform, and carbol, which now and then filled me with nausea.

It seemed to me that the vehicle didn't move from its spot, as if it was rattling in place.

But after half an hour I had the feeling that we were going through a forest.

I only hoped we didn't run into any trees.

The car stopped with a jolt and I was thrown from the pillows.

The driver opened the car door.

"We've broken down. Please step out."

The Albino and Hyacinth stepped out.

I got up from the stretcher. Clothed only in a shirt, I stepped out of the wagon.

The Albino and Hyacinth had disappeared. I thought nothing of it.

Darkness all around.

I walked a few steps like I was on jelly or the surface of an inflated balloon.

Perhaps the earth is a balloon that hovers in ether? I looked up and saw some stars. I began to count: one—two—three.

The stars reminded me of headlights. I looked for the lights of the ambulance in the darkness.

They had gone out.

It was as if the earth had swallowed up the car.

A muggy, oppressive atmosphere reigned.

The damp air nearly took my breath away.

It was still dark. I groped my way forward, but before me the rose-colored intimation of the day to come was already breaking through a deep cobalt blue.

I groped around—my sense of touch said to me: from tree to tree. But these trees must have been trees of a certain type:

They must have been flowing trees composed of a heavy, thick liquid because touching them was like trying to grab honey.

Finally, lightning-quick, day broke.

I stepped on soft, fragrant soil through a strange forest.

Gigantic palm trees vaulted over me.

There were trees that stood as tall as church towers—wellingtonians and eucalyptus—and a golden stream of resin flowed down constantly from their trunks. Cacti sunk their claws into heaven and earth.

A dragonfly the size of an eagle hovered over my forehead.

There was something girlish or Madonna-like about its head and I almost thought that it was Maria's head.

Madonna immaculata!

Libellula immaculata!

O golden-winged one, come tarry a while!

Before my eyes the dragonfly crumpled to its natural size and hovered, dazzling and iridescent.

I could no longer recognize her head.

Now I thought that this could be the dragonfly that was embroidered on the blonde lady's veil.

I entered a clearing.

A wild horse rose from a pit as I drew nearer. It galloped away and I saw it had twelve hooves, three on each leg.

Apes swung on vines.

They didn't notice me at all—I marched through the gigantic trees and animals like a stag beetle or a flower chafer.

"The earth" I thought quite unprompted, "belongs to you. You are indeed a dwarf, but you have something like a brain, you can think, draw logical conclusions, and with guile and cunning you can defeat these giant animals and trees."

A white, snow-covered mountain shimmered through the trees. It rose like an iris from the swamp. The closer I came, the more it seemed that prints of human or humanoid feet led up to it. Suddenly, like in a movie, black letters appeared on the face of the mountain:

Mount Everest, the Wonder of Tibet.

Heavenly father, I cried, let me experience this wonder!

And I continued on my way. The landscape revealed itself ever more wonderfully. Flora and fauna gradated one into the next with no clear delineations and it could not be determined: this is an animal, or: this is a plant. There were trees with snakes for branches and sunflowers that bore the faces of stingrays. Along the path crawled gigantic caterpillars from whose scaly limbs bloomed violets and flies with cut diamonds in place of faceted eyes flew about. A lion strolled on stone feet, his tail made of stalks of wheat.

I passed waterfalls crowned by mills of Tibetan origin. These weren't built to mill grain—they were prayer mills in which the water babbled ceaseless prayers. And wind sang through harps hung in the trees.

The higher I climbed, the less tolerable the weather's conduct became. It was at once burning hot and icy cold. I had frostbite on my feet and my head believed it was succumbing to sunstroke.

"Lord," I cried, "when will I reach the peak?"

I saw the footprints that led to the mountain: none led back.

The mills babbled.

The winds sang.

A nightingale climbed out of the brush before me. I saw it tug its way through the shining ether, singing. My heart dilated and I knew: he who leads the nightingale through the impassable air will lead my path to a good end as well.

And I walked and cried and sang into the sun—By either rubbing or smashing together pieces of flint that lay on the path I fashioned myself a club and a knife.

With these eoliths I would make my way.

XV

A HYACINTH SCENTS AND A NIGHTINGALE BEGINS TO CALL

I gripped the club tighter.

Then I heard a voice, a lovely, familiar voice.

"You're hurting me!"

I squinted at the light invading my eyes.

I held Hyacinth's hand convulsively.

Her hand: that was the club with which I would destroy my enemies.

I was lying in a bright, white-washed hospital room in a wide, comfortable bed.

I lay softly as if on clouds, on the white pillows that smelled of fresh laundry.

Hyacinth had donned a nurse's uniform,

She wore a white bonnet and under it her face shone with even more charm and authority, like the moon under a white cloud.

68

She wore a cross around her neck.

But there was nobody nailed to this cross.

These words were written upon it:

Light! Love! Life!

A sweet scent permeated the room.

"Why does it smell so sweet?"

I asked quietly and thought it must be her breath.

She pointed to the hospital table at the end of the bed.

There was a white hyacinth.

I was frightened, but in a different way than I'd been before.

It was a joyful, lovely fear.

I groped for her hand.

"What should I call you?"

"Only call me what befits my uniform. Call me: nurse."

"Which direction does my room face, nurse?"

"Do you want to see the sun rise or set?"

I parried.

"I hate the sun. The moon is my companion. The night is my friend. I can't stand the way the sun reflects off of silver knives."

The nurse caressed my forehead.

"This room faces north."

I sighed, relieved.

"How beautiful it must be at the north pole—cold—cold—the world there is as cold as my heart—and then: eternal twilight..."

Somewhere, a nightingale began to call.

I listened to it enraptured, until my delight transgressed into anxiety.

It was January—how could a nightingale sing in January?

Hyacinth had also raised her head to listen.

Then she smiled:

"There is no cause for alarm: that is the young girl in the second ward who thinks she is a nightingale."

"A girl who thinks she's a nightingale?"

"She began to hallucinate in a childbed fever and these hallucinations have still not left her. She believes that with her song she will be able to coax the little nightingale man, the father of her child."

I closed my eyes and turned pale.

I remembered the letter from the hospital.

What if it was me that the nightingale was calling?

Had I not already encountered her while strolling through the fantastic forest?

The nurse sat down on her chair and sewed a child's bonnet.

"Don't you think she sings like a real nightingale? Professor Ziegelbert, the famed ornithologist who also lives here claims that she is replicating the nightingale's song correctly to the most minute detail, even though she could have never heard a nightingale sing, having never left Berlin's stony desert."

XVI

YENKADI

THE ALBINO appeared every morning at eleven on the dot.

He noted my temperature in his chart and wrinkled his brow or belched thoughtfully.

"Yesterday evening 38.9, this morning 38. That is far too high. Have you been digesting?"

The nurse answered in my place:

"Yes."

"Pyramidon?"

"0.6"

"Dionin?"

"0.02 three times."

"Night sweats?"

"Changed his shirt twice."

"This patient should chiefly receive liquid and gelatinous foods and as cold as possible: ice-cold milk, cornflour, chicken gelatin."

"Yes, doctor."

"Blood?"

"Still present in the sputum."

If he has another fit apply an ice bag and 25 drops of syrup three times."

"Yes, doctor."

"The sputum has been examined?"

"Gaffky 5."

"Fine—goodbye."

The Albino shook my hand and patted my head gracelessly.

Since I was not allowed to read, the nurse supplied me with glue, glossy paper of every color and a pair of scissors.

And I began to cut:

First ornaments of every sort which I glued: white on black, grey on pink, or blue on gold.

Then a negro idol emerged which I hung on the wall above my bed and I prayed to him and called him:

Yenkadi.

It was a white idol: white on black.

Because black people have white idols and white people have black idols.

But Yenkadi is a word from Senegal that means:

It is good here! Here we can build huts!

Here is paradise!

The Albino laughed at Yenkadi when he saw him hanging by the bell above the bed.

"Make sure never to press Yenkadi instead of the button for the bell or else the sky might collapse..."

But Nurse Hyacinth looked at the idol with questioning eyes, as if she knew something more about him or she was waiting for an answer.

So I returned to the free shaping of my paper images. Gold, blue, silver, black, red, green, yellow looped and looped in chaotic patches, triangles, prisms, circles, arabesques, and the images that developed suggested fantastic insects, dragonflies and deep-sea fish or protozoa like I had met during my walk through the fantastic forest. Among them was an elephant who had sawfish for tusks, giant jellyfish for ears, an eel for a tail. And his eyes were two starfish.

But I also made a piece out of nothing but newspaper clippings, like "Criminal Aunt from America!" "Ladies Save Money!" "Yellow Dog Escapes!" "Foot and Mouth Disease!" "We Save Your Hair!" "Inventory sale: Universe 1921."

The images from this period looked very strange. I also cut heads from men and placed them on women's bodies and vice versa. A statesman got the beautiful legs of a dancer. Her head was placed on a hyena. The hyena's head was placed on a general.

So I played the creator.

So the devil played our dear God.

XVII

MORPHINE

THE inhaler hissed. White menthol steam flowed singing from glass trumpets. It hung in drops studded damply on the ceiling. The nurse shoved the apparatus onto me from the adjustable bedside table, supporting my ruined back with a cushion. Irregularly, interrupted by coughing fits, I sucked the hot white clouds into my oral cavity and pushed them out again. My glasses fogged up. The room dissolved with a smile. The nurse swirled like a soft cottonball balloon in a roundel of skimmed images, staggering thermometers, destemmed roses, contentless books from which the ink had been wiped away. Empty pages turned on their own accord.

"Ten minutes," said the nurse, "that's enough."

I sank down, exhaling.

The door opened mysteriously and soundlessly like a blooming rose and the Albino appeared. He arched up to the bed. His brown outfit rattled like it was made from sheet metal. His white beard hung from his chin like a cotton candy cone. His red eyes fell like soldier beetles onto the covers.

He checked my pulse with a sure fist.

"How's it going?"

The moisture on my glasses vaporized: the world showed up more clearly. Some images of beautiful women I'd loved stalked into view. One held her head in her hands as if the earth was too heavy for her to bear on her head. Another blinked cheerfully with olive eyes. Yet another held two children in her arms: a brightly clothed, delicate girl and a blond boy in a sailor's suit. She, the mother, however, still looked like a child herself and could have been mistaken for the third sibling.

My glance fell upon the yellow roses. They swayed vibrantly on their stems. The thermometer the doctor pulled out of my armpit showed a clear reading.

Life could be so torturously lapidary.

"39.1," the Albino said to the nurse, who apologized with her hips turned.

I looked at the doctor. A good man! How,

as round as a balloon, he floated about the room. He was certainly determined to extinguish the fire, to reinforce the walls so that the house would not collapse. And now he rolled up his sleeves. Reddish hairs sprouted like heather from his forearms.

He stepped up to the table, opened a case. Washed the needle of the injection apparatus with eau de cologne.

The nurse pushed the covers back and the Albino said: "Alright, please stretch out your right leg."

The needle glided painlessly into my yellow flesh which inflated slightly over the injected liquid. The Albino washed himself and floated away. The nurse covered me with the eiderdown. Then they could be heard warbling with the assistant in the hallway.

A gramophone began to rattle in the room below mine. A onestep accompanied by laughter.

I sat up, slipped out of bed and stood with trembling knees. I had stepped out of myself and now willingly stepped into the roundel of events. I came up to the long-stemmed roses on the wash table, consubstantially anxious. The central heating did not warm me, only itself. I warmed myself. The pictures on the walls, like sisters, allowed themselves to be recognized: not as embodied women but as pictures in frames, just like I was a picture in a gilded wooden frame, supported above and bellow, nailed on the wall like a murderer. For every Christ there's always a million murderers.

The gramophone chimed cheerfully like a streetcar. I dreamily entered the carriage of these tones for a long journey. I lifted my feet—I needed my hands to hold up my violet pajamas so that they wouldn't fall down and trip me. I climbed higher and higher and made it up the spiral staircase that led to the top of the streetcar. There I sat down and saw the city far below me. Smoke lay like moss above the factories. The fumes of gasoline filled the sunny air. The river shone with an exhilarating consciousness of the goal towards which it rushed. Cranes moved up and down like iron arms. An arm gestured towards heaven and then towards earth. Then to the river. Bells rang from every church. In the chorus of their songs I lifted myself from the top deck as the conductor handed me the ticket, and with my head thrown back, I moved radiantly through the air.

XVII

THE MIRACLE

I saw Potsdamer Platz and a colorful crowd moving upon it. It was the Potsdamer Platz of 1921, but the people who populated it, who climbed out of cars, trams and subways, wore Greek outfits and togas.

A Dominican monk blazed his way through the crowd, raised his voice loudly and cried:

"God greets you!"

Many people stood there in their Alexandrian outfits like they were in front of a street merchant who was selling cigarettes or oranges, and one, a boy, said: "He greets you, venerable elder—if we mean the same god."

The monk responded:

"Which then is your god?"

The boy spoke:

"He is the god whose temple you see there,

proud and stony."

And he gestured toward the Wertheim department store and the Café Vaterland.

The monk spoke:

There is only one God: the omnipotent, omnibenevolent, omniscient—and there is no God besides him."

The boy smiled:

"Your age prohibits me from teaching you as I would if you were younger. Let me say to you though, that I know many gods: the one from Berlin, the one from Yokohama, the one from Moscow. The one from Moscow or from Yokohama has no power over us; neither will your god, foreigner—your costume allows you to be recognized as such—be able to do anything either for or against us."

The monk spoke:

"There is only one God, revealed through his son, who descended from heaven to earth."

Then I, who had followed the conversation up to here, pushed my way through the crowd and cried to the monk:

"Hey you filthy son of an ape! Be careful I don't grab you by your dirty beard—get los with your childish lies. You might be able to convince the brainless sons of your degenerate people, bot not the boys of Berlin, who have passed through the school of wisdom. Here is the earth—there is heaven: so let your son of God come down from heaven. I see no ladder or stairs by which he could do so."

Then the crowd laughed.

The monk, however, kneeled down beneath the regulator clock.

"Lord, Lord, see me kneel before you in most heartfelt prayer. Do not allow me to become the mockery of your enemies. Light them with the torch of your wisdom and make signs and wonders, that your power and strength and the truth of my faith and my speech might be revealed. Lord, Lord, descend from Heaven and come into our hearts..."

Then heaven opened.

A staircase appeared to lead from there down to earth upon which a beautiful boy slowly descended with his arms extended in blessing. He climbed down the staircase to earth where he suddenly disappeared among the crowd and was no longer visible. And a voice struck like thunder from the clouds: "Satan—get thee gone from this place!"

And I fled sideways, my hands pressed before my face.

I still heard the screaming and shouts of the crowd:

"Where is this God, that we may worship him? He descended from heaven to earth and disappeared."

Then the voice of the monk rang like a clapper striking a bell:

"He is among you..."

XIX

THE MOONLIT NIGHT

I woke up in anxiety.

The moon shone pallid into the room and bathed the white god on his black background with its rays so that he shone like radium. His eyes, composed of two matchstick heads, gawked and he lifted his arms as if he wanted to leave the picture and climb down to me.

And then I began to fear my own creation. Yenkadi had always been in my soul. Yenkadi had only just now come into the light—and only because he wanted to. Yenkadi had witnessed my deeds and misdeeds. Yenkadi came demanding reckoning from me. Yenkadi spoke:

"Already I was, before you were, and I will be when you are no longer. Remember when you were born and opened your eyes for the first time: did I, Yenkadi, not stand there and lean over you? What has become of you, that you have forgotten me for years, for centuries—until one day you cut me out of white glossy paper—and see, I am again revealed! But I was always in you and omnipresent. I went through the forest, when first you embraced Maria among the ferns. Why would you not shout my name, the name of your god: Yenkadi: much would have been left for you.

"I pushed back the curtains of your nuptial bed. But you did not remember me. And in that night of nights, when the blood began to flow: you were silent and did not shout: 'Yenkadi! Yenkadi!'"

I felt cold sweat on my forehead.

I wanted to scream but I only managed to wheeze: "Nurse! Nurse!"

Nurse Hyacinth stood in the moonlight before me and bent over me, as once Yenkadi had bent over my crib. She had let down her blonde hair and stood there in a white blouse.

And as I saw her standing there:

I saw that it wasn't her.

It was Maria.

She stood there in a burial shroud, so silvery pale. She untied the band from her chin and dried the sweat from my forehead.

"Why do you fear me? And yourself? I am with you every day and night."

I raised my arms to the moon. The moon and her: all was one. "Have I not gone mad with longing for you, my shining one, my mild ray, my cool child? Have you returned to save me and to give my love sense and my life meaning? Come, come into my arms! Come into bed with me! Cool my burning heart with your cool breasts, my burning eyes with your lips of snow! Hold fast the torch of my fate in your good hand! Love me! Beloved nurse!"

She sat at my bedside and patted my forehead.

"There, there my ardent boy, you have a fever! And if I were to love you and you had another hemorrhage in my arms—what would the doctor say? And how would I answer for my criminal negligence?"

"Angel!" I screamed. "I martyred you— and you, you love me nonetheless and love me more than all concepts and measure."

She pressed a gentle kiss upon my lips:

"Sleep, my love, you must sleep. Speak no more. You should try to heal." And she began to sing softly:

"Sleep in sweet repose,
close your eyes and doze.
Hear the raindrops tap,
and the neighbor's puppies yap
A puppy bit the man,
and he tore the robber's pants.
The robber's gate is closed.
Sleep in sweet repose."

A dog barked somewhere in the neighborhood.

The cool hand on my forehead did me so
much good.

Somewhere a nightingale sang very softly.

Even now she sang into my dream like
sweeping pasture grass.

XX

THE FESTIVAL OF THE DEAD

TODAY was the festival of the dead. Once a year they leave the realm of the dead at the bottom of the ocean, where they make their home among coral, starfish, rays, oysters, eels and spiders. They ascend like glass jellyfish and when they reach the sea's surface, suddenly winged, they lift themselves into the air and like white swarms of herons they head in formation for solid ground, where they tumble from the clouds and take on the form that they bore when they dwelt among the living.—I, the cricket dealer Hen-Yo, had prepared everything for the arrival of my lovely spouse Ise. The house altar was decorated with white roses. I had already lit 17 candles. Because my wife, my beloved, had only reached the age of 17. My tender, fragile one had died giving birth to our first child: she had brought the child with her into the world of the dead. There he slept, dreamless under crystal shrubs and his mother watched like a stone over his sleep. The green waves surged over them both.—Bowls with rice, fruits, and little cakes were placed before the altar. Ise would be hungry from her long journey through the water and the wind. The teapot hummed. Three cups were prepared: two larger ones—they were still quite small— and a smaller one. I sat, my pointed head in my broad hand, and waited. Outside, on the doorposts, a poem fluttered on long strips of paper. I had composed it myself and painted the paper: silver signs on a black background. "Ise—return!" the poem sang.—It had grown dark. The flickering candles threw trembling shadows over the small, clay, green-glazed god who sat in the altar's niche with his legs crossed and his hands raised so that his palms stared forwards like pale lotus blossoms. He made a strict, dismissive, merciless face and seemed to grin in the twilight. The movement of his hands indicated: "Let go of your foolish hope, Hen-Yo! I, the god of your ancestors and your god, who knew of you, before you ever were and will know of you when you are no more, I say to you: Ise will never return. She will never return, just as she was never there. She is only an image, a conceit of your fantasy (which has never wanted for colorful animation). You dreamed her. You saw her and once your longing gave her a moving shape. You are too weak to create her anew. Dream a new dream! Even better: strike the gong! wake up! Do not let your being decay! You still have so much to do in life. Have you, for example, taken care of the crickets for the evening?"—I got up. I approached the rows of ornate wooden cages, in which hundreds of crickets sat. Every cricket had a cage, since they could not be locked up together. They hated each other and would eat one another. Even males and females could not last long together without the female, the stronger of the two, consuming the male. I owned only one female, whom I had inadvertently caught once with the male she was embracing. I released all the females, since only the male crickets are marketable. Only they chirp. My method of catching crickets was otherwise quite simple. All I needed was a blade of grass. I put this into the cricket holes and the crickets, who could not bear its tickling, exited and became easy prey.—Lamentations and monotone prayers rang through the thin bamboo walls of the neighboring houses. Some of the crickets began to chirp. Others joined in. I fell upon my forehead before the altar. I prayed the prayer for the dead, then the minor prayer, then I sang the litany to the melody of Autumn music. When I had finished, I saw by the light of a candle a black cricket sitting on a white hyacinth. In my negligence, I must have left a cage open. I took the cricket in my hand. It was the female but, O wonder, she began to chirp, and as I listened more closely, I heard her speaking, fine and softly. "I am Ise. I am always with you in my second form. We the dead can take on a doubled shape: dwell both in the realm of the dead and the realm of the living. But the living know nothing of this. Only once a year do we allow ourselves to be recognized, when you celebrate with us the festival of the white hyacinth. I have always been with you. You just did not know it. You brought me nourishment every morning and evening: fresh spring water and tender, green stalks. I am your only cricket female and you have taken gentle care of me. Today you shall receive your reward." The black scales on the back of the cricket raised like the trapdoor of a dungeon vault and broke off: and she hovered from the prison of the animal's body, shimmering, light as wind and transparent as glass: Ise, as I had seen her once, when she still lived. She stood there before me, just as magical as in my memory. She wore a blue kimono embroidered with sunflowers and she held the boy, who appeared to sleep, in her arms. We bowed low before the altar. We bowed before the gawking god three times, putting our foreheads to the floor. My heart trembled before this blessedness like a winch in the wind. I poured tea. I offered rice, sweets, candied fruits. I was unable to speak. My lips lay like plates of stone, one upon the other. The god in the background had drawn into himself. His green eyes shone. He meditated.—When we had silently drunk our tea, Ise placed the god into the arms of the child. Then she turned to me, embraced me weakly and drew me to the marital bed; the mats lay in the corner, just as they once had. We sank into bliss without words. The chirping of crickets sounded in our love. Finally I found the words: "Stay with me, Ise! Do not leave me! I could not bear it!" Ise shook her head and her high blonde hair, out of which protruded tortoise shell combs, leaned forward. "I cannot stay with you, Hen-Yo, as a being of your kind. As a cricket, yes, or as a star or a cloud. You must stay with me, Hen-Yo. Go with me over the rainbow bridge. Find the way that will unite us forever." I spoke: "Is it not the same, whether you stay with me or I stay with you?" Ise stared at me, surprised. Her eyes now had the color and greenish shine of the god's eyes. She was silent. The candles burned down. Midnight, the hour of the dead's departure, came nearer. Ise spoke: "Is everything prepared for my voyage home, as has been the custom since time immemorial?" Then I sighed deeply, tears in my eyes. "I have acted in accordance with the law of gods and ancestors." And I pushed open the sliding door to the garden. A stream bordered it. A white paper ship with a candle for its mast lay on a mahogany table in an arbor. The stream was already sown and starred with such ships, upon which the souls of the dead traveled homeward, downstream, into the great sea. Thousands and thousands glided down the quiet flow. The candles blinked. The lamentations from the shore resounded after them. Then Ise spoke: "You left a boat on the jetty that you use to fish from time to time. Come travel with me back to the realm of the dead and stay with me! Take me with you in your boat!" So I let the paper boat go downstream without a candle, where it struck another, caught fire, and sank. I let go of the chain and Ise, the child in her arm, jumped into the boat and set herself at the bow. I bound the holy candle to the mast, lit it and gripped the rudder. And the barge glided down to the sea.

92

XXI

WHEN THE LITTLE BELL RINGS.—THE DOOR WITHOUT A HANDLE

THE next morning I found myself run aground upon my bed.

Hyacinth held the picture of Maria in her hand.

She considered it with tender attention.

But she and the figure in the picture seemed so similar to me that I could not know: was the picture looking at her or was she looking at the picture?

Until I remembered that the picture couldn't see because it had no eyes.

Because I took them out.

In rage. In indignation. In fear. In evil.

And I dreaded and was ashamed of myself.

"She must have been such a wonderful woman!" Said Hyacinth, "Stable. Harmoniously vaulted like Michelangelo's dome at St. Peter's in Rome, but richly decorated like Bernini's tabernacle. She smiled seriously: a Madonna by Cimabue. She blooms, a white rose on a black background, Sister of Yenkadi. A grave must be erected for her like the colossal grave of Cecilia Metella on the Apian Way before the Porta San Sebastiano in Rome. She carries the symbol of the holy trinity on her forehead: was your mother, child, and beloved."

On the wall, Yenkadi moved his lips at me: "When the three again are one, as the three once were—then you are saved."

Hyacinth spoke:

"I can't compete with this splendor. But I love you."

I straightened up:

"When will you belong to me, as you promised?"

She pressed back the hair that had welled up onto her forehead.

"When the little bell rings..."

Then she kissed me softly on my forehead:

"But most importantly you must get well, lovely man."

She looked into my eyes for a while.

I became unsure.

"Why are you scrutinizing me?"

"Because I like to look into your eyes."

I became ill at ease:

"That's not true. You're trying to discover something. You're searching for something. You don't see: you spy like a tracker on the hunt. Like a bird of prey after its victim."

"Oh, child, how funny you are!"

"If I'm funny, why don't you laugh at me as I laugh at myself?" I burst out in laughter. "I really find myself very funny."

"You have to calm down."

"You always look so strangely into my left eye. What do you see there?"

"But both of your eyes are equally dear to me."

"No, you always look into my left eye, the eye above my heart. What do you see there?"

She stared at me, surprised.

"Myself!"

So I fell back into the cushions.

"So—you—too—shall—suffer—your—fate…"

I straightened myself up again:

"But maybe you deserved it, right?"

I grew angry and harsh.

"The moonstone, which lies next to the Indian cat and the picture without eyes, has been dull for the past few days. And the marble cat has been scratched. Do you know what that means?"

She shook her head.

"That you're cheating on me! All your loving oaths are lies! And you withhold yourself from me. You're cheating on me—"

"But child, with whom?"

I screamed:

"With the Albino!"

She smiled sadly:

"My love…"

I raised myself higher:

"Oh I have proof. I discovered this just today. Why does this door have no handle? And the window has no lock? I want say this to you: I am lying helpless here in bed and maybe you're keeping me sick artificially: because you're scared that I'll follow you and walk in on your shameful dealings? Oh I see right through you. Show me your left hand. Why is it clenched into a fist? No, you don't want to hit me (though your most secret, craven desire might be to hit me, to stab me, to torture me): no, you have the latchkey in there—and whoever doesn't have the latchkey can't open the door from the inside. I am your prisoner. I have been surrendered to you, helpless and defenseless."

A crying fit convulsed me.

Hyacinth stroked my hair with a light kiss. I felt her arm.

The hyacinth on the bedside table released its scent.

"Cry, my dear, cry your eyes out. You are feverish."

XXII

AMOR AND PSYCHE

"PSYCHOANALYTIC THERAPY," said the Albino, "is pure bullshit. Garbage. Because it affords no attention to the underlying biological basis. Do you think that a man with a homosexual orientation, after someone has demonstrated to him his repressed complexes and has brought his most hidden consciousness to the surface, is healed after that? He'll pay you something for it. He remains just as homosexual as he was. He must be operated on. Gland operation. That's what will do it. Eight days later he fathered his first child with unfeigned enthusiasm. Consider Professor Steinach's experiments on rats. He gave male rats female sex glands and vice versa. And their "spiritual life" reversed automatically. A male rat took on female mannerisms and tendencies and a female rat took on male traits. I am a Marxist. Psyche here reflects culture in general. The psyche is only the superstructure built upon the physical base, culture is the superstructure upon the economic base."

I decided to try and contribute:

"Well no matter what, you have to know something about psychoanalysis to understand art these days."

The Albino knit his brow. His red eyes became even redder. "Oh yeah, good—art. As soon as you can stand up—show me your pulse: great; and your temperature? Excellent—as said, I grant you permission to make visits to Ward Roman Numeral Three. There you will find within a few square meters of space the works of Goethe, Schiller, Böcklin, Manet and Monet, Pindar and Hölderlin, Kokoschka and Picasso, to your heart's content. And the whole rest of the cultural superstructure is richly represented: the works of Loyola, witches, monks, sphinxes, exorcists, samurais, Freemasons, Princes of Hell—whatever you want. Even our dear God is present in person and issues audiences from 2 to 4. Unfortunately medical science is not quite there yet: but one day it will get there: all you need to do is operate on people—then they'll be utterly useful. I am in favor of operating and giving shots. That is the entire medical wisdom. Surgery! Chemistry! If you are ever too far gone I will inject you with some tuberculin so that your hearing and vision go away."

Nurse Hyacinth laughed at his grim face. She knew that one shouldn't come to the Albino with psychoanalysis: he goes wild. That was his complex. When he left the room, I also laughed.

"You see what I mean?" We only used *du* when we were alone—"Today is a wonderful, beautiful day. Today you laughed for the first time! And you can also stand! You'll get a rubber-tipped cane, a latchkey that will open the door, and you'll be able to make visits around the hospital."

"I still hear the nightingale singing. I have to go to her first—if I can get her out of the cage—"

"For the time being you're still in a cage", teased Hyacinth.

A vein in my forehead throbbed.

"Now, now," she kissed the vein which disappeared under her lips.

"I didn't mean for that to come out so bad..."

XXIII

THE TRINITY

THERE was a knock.

Hyacinth opened the door.

And a strange procession stepped inside.

At the front strode an honorable old gentleman with a white cotton beard and gleaming, beautiful eyes. He wore a woman's nightgown made from red fleece and upon his head was a pointy merchant's cap that was covered in golden stars. In his one hand he held a cage, in which a home had been made for a white Barbary dove, and in his other hand was a beautiful boy in a roman tunic, around whose neck was tied a wooden cross.

Behind the cross strode a hasidic rabbi in a black kaftan, who was murmuring secret prayers and agitating the upper half of his body ecstatically. An older Prussian General, his Excellence, hobbled on a Frederician cane, supported on his left by an aristocratic gentleman, who wore a bugle, and on his right by a dancer made up like a harlequin.

They were followed closely by a couple of newlyweds, she wearing a myrtle wreath, and he—a top-hat.

He moved himself forward on crutches.

Her knees shook.

He was 105, and his bride was 91.

"My love," whispered her toothless lips.

"My sweet," echoed the old man.

He adjusted his glasses.

"I feel you are showing too much bosom. I am growing jealous."

"And you are flirting with the nurse..."

"Your exquisite curves should not be visible to just anyone."

"Your glance, your heart belong to me alone."

"Do you crave me?"

"Unspeakably so."

"When will the day of our marriage be? when will our marriage night come?"

"Soon, my angel, soon."

They stepped off sideways like a backdrop, and a man in a cassock made of burlap appeared. It was the monk from Potsdamer Platz.

He gave me his visiting card straight away, upon which was written:

*Salvatore Ciavolino, ventriloquist and
exorcist, member of the lodge Axmadora,
available and highly recommended to
the honorable gentleman in need of devil
summoning.*

A man in a violet velvet jacket crept up and passed me a book bound in silk. I read the title in silver print:

*A to Z
Conversational Lexicon of the Forbidden
Sciences*

I opened the book and leafed through— white, untouched pages gawked back at me.

The book was empty.

But the theosoph made himself heard:

"The day will come! Come on down to the 'Coming Day' at D.K.T. Spiritual and Economic Worth Incorporated. Soul and business: it's all the same to us. Business is our soul, and the soul is our business! We invite you to invest! Ten million shares already sold. Buy the next million! Already in our possession are a cigar factory, a food factory, an umbrella factory, a first class hotel (into which God the Father himself is known to descend), a razor factory, a sawmill, a press publishing communist and monarchist texts, a temple, an export business, a Trappist cloister... Try our metaphysical shaving cream! You will be fabulously sudsed. Give our 'Nirvana' cigars a try. You'll be a regular customer after just one... Blow clouds of blue, of violet smoke like you can only imagine with Nirvana."

"Mister," I screamed infuriated, "please stop. Enter your Trappist cloister as soon as possible!"

The dignified old man with the cap on his head approached me:

"My name is God the Father.—This here" he indicated the boy at his side, "is my beloved son, bearing his cross. This is my *tertium comparationis*," he pointed to the dove, "the Holy Ghost in person, who as you well know is winged and a dove."

The dove in the cage began to coo and laugh and its laughter degenerated into paroxysm.

God the Father knit his brow.

"Once again—the insolence of the Holy Ghost. He makes fun of creation. But what more can one ask of an irrational animal? The Holy Ghost sh... indeed."

104

He examined the floor of the cage disapprovingly.

"But what is there to do? This is the only real, the only true Holy Ghost, and only with him and my dear son," he patted the boy, with whom he seemed to be in a homosexual relationship, "am I a complete trinity.—We have come to worship a strange God who is supposed to be spending his time in this room!"

He looked around the room, searching.

I indicated Yenkadi, who shone, white on black, from the wall.

"The god is there, unmoving—but he rules his world mightily and without error. His name is Yenkadi."

The Trinity bowed piously.

The dove wiggled its tail and forced its beak through the bars of the cage.

God the Father bowed down as he might once have learned at dance class: old fashioned, as if he wore a petticoat: as if Yenkadi were his chief clerk.

The boy was already smiling:

"I am the way, the truth, and the life: no man cometh unto the Father, but by me."

The Exorcist imitated an *ave* bell: bong—bong—bong.

God the Father, dove in hand, God the Son, the theosoph, the newlyweds all kneeled down and crossed themselves.

The hasidic rabbi davened.
The dancer danced.
His excellence saluted.
The aristocrat of the old gentry blew the
hymn "Praise the Lord" on his bugle.
Twilight fell in the room.
Hyacinth held her hands in prayer as well.
Yenkadi shone white on black.
Then I too folded my hands.

XXIV

DICTATOR MUNDI

ONE day, and it came as a bit of a surprise, Munk came to visit me. It must have been a long journey from Ganselache over Krausnickstrasse and into my hospital room: he was dressed with an obnoxious, repulsive elegance that stood in stark contrast to his hitherto proletarian existence.

He addressed me with *du* immediately.

"I read about your illness in the paper. The shared memories of our schoolboy days render it my duty to look after you."

I remembered a Pentecost trip into Birkenwald. We shook maybugs: how numb they fell from the trees: the bakers and cobblers and princes and kaisers: when we shook the trees—before sunrise.

Munk removed his lemon-yellow gloves. "I shook the world tree and Odin's oak: before sundown. Then they fell from the stalk: the grain princes, the coal barons, the iron counts, the emperors. I was the first chairman of a revolutionary club. When I struck the table with my fist the glasses and palaces of the mighty began to wobble. We rebelled. We sang the Marseillaise. I determined that in days to come the sun would again have to turn around the earth. We decided accordingly.

"I inaugurated free love when late at night at Gruener Weg on Father Grumbkow's sofa I exemplified *coitus interruptus* on the living subject of Maria the waitress. And yet I still impregnated her. So she conceived and bore Christian, my son and adversary, immaculately. He is now seventeen years old and has been taken in by this institution where he appears to be in a remarkable relationship with a certain God the Father. He has taken on the title God the Son."

"I got to know him a couple days ago. He made a very sympathetic impression on me."

Munk whinnied.

"Look at you!"

He lit a "Nirvana" brand cigar, neglecting to offer me one:

"He's a dangerous boy. Suspect and antirevolutionary. He's in protective custody here."

I coughed in the cigar smoke:

"But what did he do?"

"That's just it: he didn't do anything. That is a crime in this most active of times. It wants to move forward: and he's falling beneath the wheels."

"You speak such grand phrases. What's become of you and what have you become?"

Munk tapped the ash from his cigar on the bedside rug:

"*Dictator mundi.* You've been living under a rock? Have you never heard of me?"

"Not since we lost contact—although I've dreamed of you, you my alter ego. So you're *Dictator mundi*—I only made it to *cursor mundi*..."

Munk opened his mouth like a devilfish.

"I am shocked and my inborn vanity is appalled. There is someone, my alter ego no less, who does not know me, to whom the echo of my potency has not penetrated."

"Forgive me: I don't read newspapers—like you."

"What do you read?"

I was silent for a moment.

"The stars and my palm."

Munk stretched his butcher's paw to me:

"Will you read my fate from my palm?"

"Show me your hand—no, the right one, not the left: the left is indomitable…"

"I rule the world and myself. I am the first servant of my utopia."

"Strong lines run to Mercury, the God of merchants. You're rich."

Munk's butcher face shone like oil.

"I live in the splendid castle Sanssouci, the former imperial residence. I have a 15% share of all state enterprises, whether they flourish or not."

"The Venusberg indicates predominantly masculine tendencies, starkly accentuated."

Flattered, Munk bowed.

"There are 15 rooms in the side wing of the castle reserved for the 15 most beautiful women of the peoples of Europe, one from each nation. Not one is older than 18 and all were virgins before I got my hands on them. This is how the peoples honor the benefactors of humanity. I effected the true League of Nations. I fertilize the virgins, each a symbol of her nation. Italy is big with child. Russia dropped twins. Mother and children are well. Germany is already in her 10th month, and there is still no sign of a coming birth."

"Your lifeline runs into a zigzag... it weaves into a hundred other lines, breaks off, starts up again. It is tainted with violence and atrocity and murder—like mine..."

Munk let his hand sink. Then he opened his arms wide: "I love humanity!"

I dared to ask:

"And how is that expressed?"

"I have compelled humanity in its own best interest."

"With what?"

"With civil war, famine, pandemic, influenza, machine guns, court martial, protective custody and the gallows."

"Are you expecting an outcry? Disgust or hymns? You too are a... human."

"Twenty million bit the dust in war and revolution. What's it good for? Humanity's happiness is on the line."

"Who is that? Humanity? I don't know her. I know me. You speak of humanity as if you love her.

But do you love any single person?"

"The individual doesn't need my love. Its place is with the collective, which I organize, paragraph, decree, socialize, communize. I decree: happiness. And a hundred million people are happy. I take the feather in my hand: Paragraph 7,315 of the intermundane legislation: poverty and crime no longer exist.—The paragraph has been confirmed by the general highest central legislative and executive committee."

"You play God, poor devil."

Munk rebuttoned his lemon-yellow glove: "If I, for the sake of old friendship, can in any way be of assistance, please. A position as assistant in the Ministry for High Art? How would that be? Hmm? Six-hour workday. Participation in the greatest artistic meetings and discussions. Visits with our great political poets. Selection of themes: brother man, the brotherhood of humanity, eternal happiness, eternal joy, man is good—these are the favorites upon which one may vary *ad libitum*. All you have to do is hum it well in a person's ear and they believe it. Man is happy when he—believes."

I contradicted:

"There is only a chemical solution to the social question. It is the only possible one because it is the only natural one. When it comes to gorging, boozing, and whoring, ethics and pseudoethics convince a person as little as any other living thing. We already produce nitrogen from the air. Once we have succeeded in converting inorganic materials to organic ones, like plants, then the social question is solved.

Hyacinth entered the room with dinner.

"Hyacinth, please allow me to introduce you: Munk, Dictator of the World, a schoolmate of mine."

Munk gawked:

"It is a great pleasure!"

Hyacinth smiled:

"It's time for you to eat supper. There's eggs, milk, and ham."

Munk rose and clicked his heels.

"The appetite stirs—and perhaps also the sexus. I am superfluous here. I'm leaving. My government car is waiting at the street bend. Do not forget to send word from time to time of my son Christian, who wants to better and save the world from the inside out and has gone a little crazy because of it. You can only reach it from the outside. The souls must be organized. The 'day to come' I think of as a really clever foundation, the primary function of which will be support. The heartbeat must be rationed. I am in favor of a Taylor system of feeling."

He brandished his stiff black hat:

"Mademoiselle!"

And to me:

"Get well soon!"

XXV

VISIT

THE dancer, the general, the aristocratic gentleman lived in a little hall next to my room. One day, the Albino granted me a visit to them. I allowed myself to be carried over in a chair by an attendant. The dancer marched like a Prussian grenadier through the little hall. One, two. One, two. The aristocratic gentleman played the Hohenfriedberger march on his bugle. His excellency, the old, white-haired general stood in a corner, examining the parade and deemed it acceptable. He wore a blue dress uniform with red piping on his green civilian pants. He produced the red piping from a discarded flag and sewed it himself. The dancer suddenly paused and only his shadow continued to march. The aristocratic gentleman set down the bugle.

The general hopped as if he were galloping with a horse under him down the front lines of a division on the battlefield. He whinnied in order to conjure the illusion of the ardent Arab stallion he fancied between his thighs. Suddenly he reigned himself in and held revue. "Gentlemen," he screamed, and his face shone cancerously red like his piping, "gentlemen, the parade march today was a disgrace..." The dancer was busy with himself. He acted as if he had taken a telephone receiver from the wall and spoke into the wall: "Miss... miss... please connect me with the northern cemetery... Is this the northern cemetery? Oh, would you be so kind as to call the late Frau Gela Krestinski to the apparatus? Yes please? Are you there my sweet? I love you, I love you more than ever... You're freezing? It was such cold, nasty weather, eh? Should I send you a blanket... that pretty Italian silk blanket?" He sobbed imperceptibly. The aristocratic gentleman, who had only heard the word "Italy," started to play *"Du mein Sorrent!"* on his bugle. Thick tears dropped from the general's eyelashes. The door, which showed no internal handle, sprung softly open, and a man in a blue and white striped apron appeared with a tray. "Food, gentlemen!" The aristocratic gentleman, hoggish as ever, lunged for the steaming bowls. The general, even greedier than he, though more disciplined, followed with measured steps. But the dancer remained at the window. He wrote "Gela" with a pointed finger on the glass. Outside in the snow a raven danced. The dancer tried to imitate the stalking, hopping animal. He stepped the first figures of his raven dance, which later, after many years, would number among his most famous. "Herr Krestinski," said the man in the blue and white striped apron, "the food is getting cold!" Then he shrugged and left. The aristocratic gentleman chewed with fat cheeks. The general crunched a roasted chicken with his gnashing jaws, bones, joints and all. The dancer still danced at the window with his partner, the raven.

XXVI

THE MATERNITY WARD

SUPPORTED by Hyacinth, I headed off to visit the maternity ward.

We stepped through a tangle of hallways like we were in one of those fairground booths with labyrinth in its name.

Screams showed us the way.

They waxed and waned, ebbed and flowed.

Finally, we had arrived.

Ward 28.

Two slogans over the entrance:

What God does is well done.

and

Suffer the little children to come unto me!

Hyacinth opened the door.

The illegitimate mothers lay in long rows, always eight to a row; little boxes stood at the footboards, and in them lay their children squealing and screeching: red like crabs or white like pale mice. Sometimes two squirmed in a single box. One side of the hall ended in an operating theatre and the other was bordered by the few rooms containing single beds. The nightingale sang in one of these.

I opened the door quietly.

A girl who was barely sixteen years old, herself still half a child, lay in the room.

It was Marianne.

She had closed her eyes.

Two long, thick blonde braids hung off the bed, almost reaching the floor.

The child in the little box slept.

You could hear its breathing regularly.

The Exorcist sat at her bed.

For a moment he desisted from the waves of Latin phrases emanating from his lips and turned to me:

"She is possessed by the devil! The nightingale that sings from her is the devil!"

Then he began to summon the devil again:

"*Propter quam causam ingressus es in corpus huius virginis?*"

And a dull voice that seemed to speak from the inside the girl answered:

"*Amoris causa.*"

"*Per quod pactum?*"

The voice in the girl hesitated:

"*Per animal.*"

The Exorcist pressed her:

"*Qualis?*"

"*Luscinia.*"

"*Quis misit?*"

The voice in the woman hesitated again.

"*Markus.*"

I held my breath.

Markus is my first name.

The Exorcist inquired further:

"*Dic cognomen!*"

The voice was silent. She did not seem to want to betray the name.

He repeated the question.

"*Dic cognomen!*"

Then, softly, she spoke my name...

The Exorcist sprang from the bed.

He brandished the cross at me:

"Ach! that it has finally come to light! Disgusting! You are the devil in the very flesh! Satanas! Pluto, Prince of Hell, sent you out to seduce and degrade this girl. Remember how you came before his throne, bent your knee over which the red cloak was billowing and spoke to Pluto: 'I have been given word of a girl called Marianne. She is gentle and beautiful beyond compare. Her will desires good, but her youth is burdened by ideas, wishes, and thoughts. She is wax in the hand of a decided former. A great desire has befallen me to possess this soul and to call it completely my own.' Then you bent your knee and the red cloak rustled: 'I will fail in my seduction. Pluto will praise his most humble servant.'—The unfortunate woman has been possessed by you. You sent her the nightingale. She unconsciously spoke your name, which for all too long her lips have silenced out of shame, compelled by this solemn exorcism. And this child that lies here in the cradle in the deepest sleep, innocent, not knowing the fate that stands before him: he is a child of the devil, he is your child..."

Hyacinth went white before the fanaticism of his speech. He swung the cross at me.

I collapsed by the bed, before the cradle.

"Yes, I admit it, I scream my admission out: I am the devil. I have murdered beauty and goodness, disgraced chastity and meekness. I am not worthy of being loved by this being, not worthy of Maria holding me in her arms, of Hyacinth becoming pale and blushing on my account...."

The Exorcist swung his cross again.

"*Adora Deum tuum, creatorem tuum!*"

And I sang from the bottom of my heart:

"*Adoro, adoro...*"

XXVII

CONSISTENCY OPENS
THE DOOR

SUNK into myself, I prayed at the cradle as I hadn't prayed since childhood.

When I stood up from the prayer—rising spiritually as well—the Exorcist and Hyacinth had disappeared.

I sat down on the edge of the bed and took the sleeping girl's hand in mine.

I don't know how long I sat like that.

All of a sudden the child became agitated.

It awoke, moved its legs, grimaced as though it had been dipped in vinegar, and cried quietly to itself.

In an instant the mother was also awake.

She looked at me with large, surprised eyes—it was as if she'd awakened from a deep dream.

Spring air wafted through the half-open window.

She looked at me again—and recognized me.

Wordlessly she wrapped her arms around me.

The child cried.

She freed herself.

"Give me the child, my love, he's hungry."

I lifted the wriggling bundle from the cradle.

She slipped her shirt off her left breast.

A magical happiness coursed through me as I laid the child on her breast.

On tip-toe, I left mother and child, just as both, exhausted from reception and concession, fell asleep.

I went past the Exorcist's room (I recognized it by the sign of the cross, of the fish, of the dove) and an untamable desire compelled me to say good night to him, since I feared that otherwise my night would be unpleasant.

I knocked.

Just as I knocked for the third time the door opened and a voice spoke:

> For he who knocks once—silent is my
>   heart,
> For he who knocks twice, my ear listens
> He who knocks thrice is heard.
> Consistency opens the door.

And I spoke:

> My finger did not make a sound
> no—my heart on the door did pound.

The voice replied:

> Come in and swing the hammer,
> and I will gladly be your anvil.

I came all the way in.

The Exorcist approached me with his arms wide: "I welcome you, brother, who hath stumbled from the path, and am grateful that you have come!"

He led me to his table.

A second placesetting lay next to his own: a tin dish with bread, a tin jug with water.

"Sit down, brother, and take part in my meal. I am always prepared for a guest. You want to know how I became who I am—since you are on the path of becoming who you are—so hear! my path was once as crooked and thorny as your own. My name is Fra Salvatore Ciavolino. I was the son of a Neapolitan cake maker and began by stealing sweets from my father. I was placed in a Dominican cloister where the Dominicans commissioned me to smuggle out their love letters. I used the money that I received from the women to buy the love of milk-maids. Then one of my beloveds cheated on me with a bersagliere and I switched over from the Dominicans to the Franciscans, became a monk, a padre, then finally a lenten preacher. I enchanted all of Naples: through my eloquence (on par with that of Demosthenes), through my youth, my beauty. The women especially fell into the net of my glances, but also tender boys, for whom I interpreted the secret meaning of life (as I then understood it) in the confession box. You could say I bore two faces: by day a pious and humble monk, and by night a brazen, horny goat, who hopped around in the bordellos and who did not disdain to prostitute himself to the manwhores. My life escaped me in a stream of lies and vices—until one day I was saved, as you too shall be saved... Confrater."

I held my breath.

"It was in one of the bordellos of the upper city, when, on the feast of Corpus Christi the holy Virgin herself relinquished her body to me in the guise of a whore and saved me as she kneeled before me, the lowest of the low, in the dust. A stream of tears flooded from me that washed all my vices away. I summoned the devil in me and went into my third cloister: this one..."

He kneeled before me:

"Issue to me your blessing and continue on your way in peace."

XXVIII

ON SENSE

THE whole night through I read an epistle that the Exorcist had given me to take along. He had written it in painfully accurate calligraphy, but he wrote the title in a rounded hand:

ON SENSE

Sense is father and mother of all things.
It begets and births in one.
It has neither beginning nor end.
It senses eternally.

According to its qualities:
according to its ONEness,
    ONEsidedness, lONEliness

—its ONEness is thought,
    its lONEliness is beheld,
    its ONEsidedness is felt by the
        faithful—it is not
desired that it should become a second,
    another.
It only wants itself.
Thus it does not deal.
And thus it does nothing .
Rather: it senses itself eternally.
It senses: neither after nor before:
    it senses.

Souls participate in sense.

They are SENSible. In this sense: that the best rePOSES in it, while the most evil still LIVES outside of it.

Sense is, to speak mathematically, comparable to a burning sphere, just like the sun.

Souls are comparable to smaller spheres, who receive their light from the great sphere, just like the stars.

Just as the stars of a solar system must one day sink into the sun, so too must souls, if they desire to be saved, someday FOUNDer in sense.

Souls and sense are eccentric spheres that constantly approach concentric spheres. First

the souls hover, only weakly illuminated, outside of the flaming sphere.

This can be presented mathematically
thus: (Fig. 1)

They con-
verge on the
great SENSE as
they reFLECT. If
we gaze from the
vantage point of
that which we
call our being
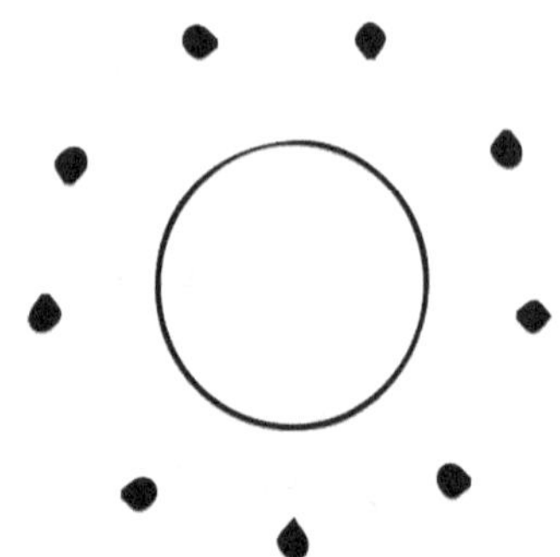
upon these phenomena, we find ourselves,
in terms of the aforementioned presentation
of our spiritual connections to sense, still in
a state of PREEXISTENCE. BIRTH occurs
at the moment when the great, conceptually
immaterial but simultaneously gaseous sphere
is touched by one of the smaller spheres.

From the very moment of birth the soul
begins little by little to become aware of ITS
SENSE. It steps into the circle of SENSE.
In the beginning its larger part lies outside
of SENSE in half-darkness as a sphere-

segment: (Fig. 2)

The more the soul suc-
ceeds in bringing this segment over into the bright
sphere, the more it will be

SENSibly aware of it. It will be illuminated with sense. The second illumination occurs at the moment of death. Here begins the third existence, the third corporeal life (the first corporeal life lies before birth, the second is this existence). This second illumination is figured as follows: (Fig. 3).

The little spheres hover, but still as eccentric spheres, within the great sphere. This third existence is ended by 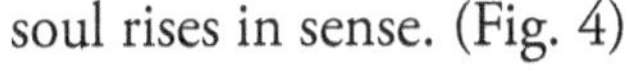 a third death (birth is the first, the so called death of the second death): if the little sphere and the great sphere become concentric, i.e., if they have the same middle point, i.e., if the soul rises in sense. (Fig. 4)

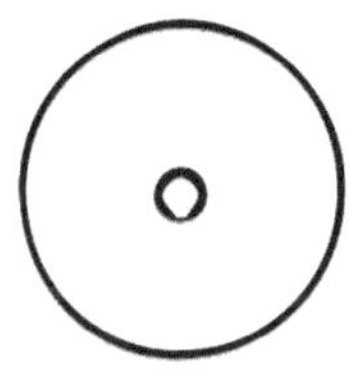 From that which has been stated, it clearly follows that SOUL and CONSCIOUSNESS are not to be identified. In the state of preexistence, the soul is still not aware of itself, wherefore we too have taken no such remembrance into this existence. Regardless, it is already present. In this life, too, the soul becomes aware of itself gradually and cautiously. The greatest part of its (spiritual) life, however, also in this life plays out external to CONSCIOUSness, in the superconscious-

ness, as it were. Only at the moment of death, when it joins the circle of sense, does the soul become for the first time aware of its own strength. It will also reflect upon itself, in order finally, once it is totally SUN-DRENCHED, to enter into the heart of the world: blessed and saved. This is the sense of sense:

The soul is slung like a boomerang from the middle-point in order to operate SENSibly, and returns—but like the boomerang only when it has met its goal!—back to the middle point.

If it operates unSENSibly, then it will hover around the great sphere outside in gloomy space, only touched by a weak gleam. But since even the most SENSEless soul retains a spark of sense from its genesis, it too is eventually permitted to contact the circle.

Sense is the end and the subversion of the soul.

The little spark is conscience.

The conscience indicates to the soul whether it proceeds properly on its orbit. The conscience alone engenders the circumstance of immortality, the eternity of the soul. Not knowledge, since that it is bound to the brain, to something corporeal, just as the intellect is something INessential. That which is essential is this: to be SENSibly illuminated. But that means: to be credulous, soft, tender, and pure: to possess great love.

It would be SENSEless, and that would be a logical fallacy, since sense cannot be SENSEless, cannot: NOT-BE-ITSELF— (since blessedness is the end of souls: to repose in sense, in God)—were this tortuous life to come to an end. This life would be a lie, a blasphemy against God himself, were it not SENSible in view of the eternal end. To what end is the beautiful man beautiful, if he is already beautiful enough to repose in his tomb? To what end is the good man good, if he is blistered and whipped for it? Why should the wicked man not be wicked, if with this he cultivates an easy life and this life indeed sinks into nothingness? No: the GOOD is immanent and the BEAUTIFUL is immanent. Only WICKEDNESS will be cast off from the spheres whirling around themselves.

Just as the spheres of the soul unite with the great sphere, so too can they separate from one another and rise up into each other. Their good and illuminating aspects attract each other reciprocally, but what is dark and evil repels. If two souls are to unite completely, i.e. they are to turn from eccentric to concentric spheres: this can only be effected through the magic of great love. This love can only be a SENSible love. If it is mere affection or appreciation, the spheres will be cut off from each other. Sensible love anticipates the process of the eventual unification of the soul with sense and it is the most beautiful and magnificent ALLegory of God, of sense in general.

With this I let the page sink.
I was unable to suppress a tear.
I thought of Maria, of Marianne, of
    Hyacinth: of the propitious trinity
    of Eros.

The soul becomes SENSible through understanding.
Love is borne upon understanding.
The highest love upon the highest understanding.

The conscience is the yardstick of understanding.

The soul desires to become good intrinsically (not extrinsically).

The sense of the souls moves towards being—not towards good deeds.

Since these only occur in the presence of people.

So that even the best agent is in vanity reflected.

No other sort of external impeachment: murder or rape: can harm the soul even in the slightest.

I had murdered Maria, raped Marianne: but their souls remained soft, tender, pure, and credulous since they possessed great love. But I only possessed great hatred.

The soul is inside.

It is borne UPON ITSELF and thus UPON SENSE. That which surrounds it is its body. And this body is air for it, just as air surrounds the earth. Its core is invulnerable. This body is air for it. Already good enough for a bird to float in. Since this was not there previously, so too later, logically, it will not be there. That which has a beginning also has an end.

But the soul is endless and without beginning.

The dagger of the enemy strikes as though through a body of aether into nothing when he seeks to kill the wise man. The claw of the tiger finds no flesh on him. The more we win sense (the only victory that lasts), the more unconscious we become of our bodies, the more conscious the soul becomes. Spinoza says: bliss is not the reward of virtue, but virtue itself. The soul is the only real thing we have. And its works alone and its consequence alone shall remain.

The conscience demands perfection relentlessly. And he who hears not its voice or desires not to hear—his soul will float with the dark spheres for a long while yet.

The wise man however can obtain the first bliss here already when he lives CONSCIONably. The kingdom of this life can only be reached in the highest understanding of sense: of love: when two SOULSTARS sublimate in flames of pure fire into a single star which shoots toward the MIDDLE POINT, rejoicing.

XXIX

THE DAY HAS COME

I spent a sleepless night poring over the wonderful, childishly foolish and greyly truthful, mathematical and mystagogical manuscript of the mad monk. Whether I wanted to or not: I felt myself deeply touched by many of his words. They struck my fate like an arrow.

Dawn began to break.

I awaited Hyacinth with desire.

When she didn't arrive at the usual time I became uneasy.

I rang for the bath attendant.

He shrugged his shoulders.

I rang for the maid.

She played with her apron, embarrassed.

"Maybe she isn't well..."

Finally, punctual as ever, the Albino entered. His face was overflowing like overcooked milk, in which his red eyes swam like tomatoes.

He was completely disoriented and bewildered.

I approached him—despair gave me strength—and shook him by the shoulders.

"Where is Hyacinth?"

My voice trembled.

He stared at me:

"Please calm down, she is here."

He paced with his hands crossed behind his back.

I fell heavily into a chair.

I sensed that something had happened, perhaps even more horrifying than everything that I had experienced up to now.

The Albino stopped before my chair with an automatic movement.

Distracted, he felt my pulse.

He stared in my eyes again.

"You are guilty on all counts. Hyacinth, too, is on your conscience."

I turned ashen.

"What are you talking about? Please continue, doctor, do not stretch me upon the rack: is—Hyacinth—still—alive?"

He was silent for a moment.

"She no longer lives—and yet she lives."

I could no longer bring word past my lips.

He explained:

"Yesterday she left the Nightingale's room with a mad smile on her face. When she reached the first men's ward, where the food had just been distributed, she halted in the middle and all at once tore the clothing from her body and, half dancing, half striding, she contorted her naked body. Her face was transfigured heavenly. She opened her arms wide, as if offering herself to one and all and spoke: This is my body! Take ye and eat ye thereof!

The patients sat stiff as mannequins in their beds. They held their breath and no one dared to move. Then she began to stride through the hall and struck up a song:

"Yenkadi! How sweet is life and heaven everywhere on earth! Come to me all ye who are belabored and encumbered! Toss away your worry, your pains, your sickness with your clothing. Yenkadi wants you naked! For divinity is naked and beauty is naked and truth is naked.

"Yenkadi!
At last the day is come!
The gloomy twilight's done!
The night has melted from
the shining rays of sun!
Yenkadi!"

And she strode singing, incanting through all the men's wards.

And the men threw off their blue hospital gowns and followed in her long procession like a troop of caterpillars and eventually everyone sang the song she sang:

"Yenkadi!
The day is come!"

The Albino was inflamed by his own story. His eyes seemed to drip blood. He stopped suddenly, like a conductor tapping his baton in the middle of a symphony, and remained standing before me: "The symptoms with which Hyacinth presented appear occasionally among hysterical women after attempts at moral assassination and attempted rape."

He took another step towards me:

"Did you attempt to rape Hyacinth?"

I held my head in my hand. It felt like it had become as heavy as a ball of lead. Oh, if only like a scorpion I had no, but instead a stinger that could protect me.

Was I crazy? Was he? What did this red-eyed medical idiot want?

"Go to the devil!" I jumped up, "or to the Exorcist! Do you not know that I love Hyacinth?"

The Albino smirked:

"I too love Hyacinth, and have likely longer than you. Your defense is ridiculous."

"Go on!" I cried, "what did—what did they do to Hyacinth?"

The Albino:

"She led this procession of the naked up through the corridors of the cloister. You know: our institution was once a Cistercian cloister. It looked horrible, the procession, I can assure you of that: all these naked, rickety, scrofulous, bloated or stick-thin bodies—I saw them behind the frosted-glass panes of my office where I hid in fear of riot, rebellion, revolt." He paused and chuckled to himself like a faucet that had been left running:

"Well, that's already over with. The uprising has been crushed. But to continue: Hyacinth was beautiful, angelic, divine to look upon. It was a balmy spring evening. She led the procession onto the court, since she found all the doors that would lead to freedom locked. It would have all turned into one big joke—the renown of my institution and my reputation as a doctor *seraphicus psychopathicus heidi*— if the procession had managed to land on Potsdamer Platz. In the courtyard Hyacinth mounted the Neptune fountain and dusk and darkness sank. She lay in the fountain's shell like a white pearl. The procession of the naked made camp around her. I observed how, as if influenced by the night, her exaltation abated. She fell asleep. And hundreds fell asleep with her."

He paused.

"I climbed quietly over the sleepers and took the sleeping woman in my arms."

I clenched my fist.

"She slept so gently. And her beauty was like that of a Greek goddess. I carried her into the warm-water chamber and laid her down on the leather sofa. To help her rest I administered an injection of scopolamine.— We quickly dominated the now leaderless procession. We drove it back into the wards with whips."

He blew air through his nose.

"Would you like to see Hyacinth?"

Hobbling, I followed him through the cloister corridors. He opened the warm-water chamber with his secret key that fit all locks. Hyacinth played in the little white-tiled tub.

She let the water trickle down her shoulders, held her breasts with her hands, then suddenly clapped.

She laughed loudly upon seeing us, a laughter that cut my heart like a knife.

Then she splashed us with water:

"You fauns! Leave me in peace! Go into the forest and play with the centaurs."

The Albino whispered:

"She does not recognize us. She thinks she's a nymph. Hmm, perhaps only an acute psychosis, a sort of nymphomania that will again subside. For years she's had to deal with the mentally ill. Most recently with yourself."

We left the cabinet.

I had to hold myself back from punching him in his disgusting rabbit face.

"I won't stand for this diagnosis."

"Well," he deflected, "I did not mean to imply that you are mentally ill—although meningitis tuberculosa is certainly relevant—I only said that Hyacinth recently had some dealings with you and cared for you. With what success we can plainly see. You are healthy—but she has gone mad."

We stopped in front of my door.

It closed with a bang:

Once again I was alone.

XXX

THE LITTLE BELL RINGS

THE next morning the bath attendant brought me a letter written in pencil.
It was strangely heavy in my hand.
It was an unfamiliar woman's handwriting.
I cut it and broke the seal.
A metal crimes unit police badge fell out.
A number was punched on it:

No. 13

and on the other side:

Homicide squad of the Royal Police
Headquarters.

I knew that I was done for.
The police were hard on my heels.

Well I was ready and prepared.

When the nightingale flew through the window, when I placed the child on the virgin breast of Marianne, who was still half a child herself, when the Exorcist summoned the devil in me, I came to a decision: to expiate my sin against Maria, to bring myself to trial, and to bear the punishment that society would impose upon me with humility and dignity.

And I read the letter:

Dear Friend!

I am not the person you think I am. When I heard your unguarded confession at the bed of the woman who had just given birth and your desire for penitence; yes, you were the penitence itself: the sin without sin—all at once I felt my indelible guilt burning.

I was your nurse, and I deceived you from the very first days of my nursing and indeed even before. Yes and even more so: I deceived you with my love, feigned and simulated my love for you, and committed the most evil act one person can commit upon another. I believed I was doing my duty to God and mankind—and

I was satisfied to follow the orders of a rotten and degenerate society that attempts to free itself of the pathetic and pitiable robbers and murderers whom it bred and raised itself by letting slip bloodhounds to follow their trail.

I was one such bloodhound, a she-bloodhound, let slip to follow your trail, because society, spurred on by denunciation, demanded your head.

I was supposed to convict you; revolutionary activities like the murder of your wife.

I was supposed to create evidence, indications, it didn't matter what, spy on your day and your night, your dreams and your feverish fantasies. I was supposed to, if it came down to it, give myself to you and loose your lips with poisoned kisses.

You are a murderer—perhaps—but a murderer without a crime. The murder that occurred, occurred without an agent. Unless the agent was God. He allowed Cain to smite Abel and for his son to be nailed to the cross.

But I am worse than a murderer.

I deceived you with my love—until, one day, I learned to truly love you.

They demanded your head but I found your heart.

I was supposed to play Judith but, because I played her poorly, I am losing my own head and Holofernes will bear your own on his shoulders for a while yet.

When I recognized my unforgivable sin against you I stumbled out of the room where a suffering woman just like me was lying, in which the Exorcist—a vulgar charlatan and profound sensitive like us all—had summoned you. I stumbled out, my heart broken and my brain seized by fiery fever.

The fever left me today.

I know what I have to do.

I was misled.

You have put me on the right path.

I am grateful.

Come to me one final time in Room 13 this evening, when the little bell rings.

Hyacinth.

And a torn calling card lay in the envelope. I put the halves together and read:

Eva Zumbusch,
Detective,
Crimes Unit III

The tears I cried were tears of joy.

I lost a nurse and a beloved—and found her again in purer, nobler form.

I waited all day for the bells to give their sign.

Just before nine in the evening the bells began to sound. And I went through the half-lit corridors.

My body cast threatening shadows on the wall and I feared them: devil rabbits, gorillas, gigantic kangaroos, cavemen, animals from the fantastic forest.

I tried the handle of No. 13 without knocking.

There lay Hyacinth, still and blonde and as beautiful as ever. An unearthly smile bloomed upon her pale face like a white hyacinth. It smelled like hyacinths.

I tip-toed up to her: "Hyacinth," I whispered, "you summoned me and here I am."

She didn't answer. Only her smile answered.

146

I grabbed hold of her hand which hung over the side of the bed.

She was as cold as when she held my hand in the ambulance.

I kissed her lips: for the first and last time.

The death knells rang unceasingly.

Outside in the park, a nightingale sang.

XXXI

THE UNMASKED GOD

I only learned this later on, but Marianne fled the hospital with her child that very night.

The attendant had neglected to close the window of her first-floor room with his patent key.

Was she the nightingale that sang in the garden as the death knells sounded?

When I returned to my room in despair, the picture without eyes had eyes again.

They were the eyes of Maria and Hyacinth: I could no longer distinguish between them since neither shone with life any longer.

The moonstone, which in the past few days had seemed dull, shone again, pure and clear.

The crack in the little Indian marble cat had also disappeared.

My glance fell upon Yenkadi.

And I mocked him:

"Yenkadi! Yenkadi! We have paradise on earth! How happily do humans live—without pain—without heart—without want—without death—we live so blessedly. Day and night are one and sun and moon are the torches of our stronghold. We love each other innocently. Our lips speak crystalline truth. Our hands intertwine in a roundel and our song praises the brothers and the sisters: the holy Hyacinth and the pious bunny rabbit with his soft red eyes, the nightingale singing so sweetly and Maria: the wreath of stars.

"Yenkadi," I cried, "I created you, god, and you betrayed me on the first day you were supposed to prove yourself. Where's your omnipotence, you big-mouthed idol? Where's your omnipresence? Your omniscience?

"Hyacinth died.

"You let her lovely life-breath evaporate as if it were the thin smoke of a burnt offering as it climbs to heaven on your altars: produced from dry brush sparked by your childish magicians and unknowing medicine-men, your dire priests. Hyacinth smiled even in death.

"But you smirk like Prinz Karneval on Ash Tuesday. Marianne has fled with her child—my child—you let it happen.

"Now I must seek her in the world.

"You are unmasked, you empty face, paper braggart.

"The Indian cat is mightier than you.

"I will replace you with Maria's image with Hyacinth's eyes and pray to her: the bipartite goddess. But you: cursed be you and outcast, ridiculed and annihilated totally."

I tore Yenkadi from the wall, struck a match—in a second he went up in flames.

XXXII

THE HEARING

I alone knew that Hyacinth had found death at her own hand. But my guilt was not expiated from this world through her atonement, even if she seemed to believe that through her martyr's death she took mine upon herself as Christ once did.

They thought I was a murderer.

The motive that compelled me was obvious enough: I had discovered who Hyacinth actually was; a spy, a snitch, placed on my neck like a tick.

And I had torn the tick from my flesh, thrown it to the ground and stepped on it.

Just before I'd entered room No. 13 the attendant had come to bring her a warm water bottle and had found her well.

The Albino had gone half-mad with agony.

He had loved Hyacinth.

"Murderer!" he screamed and shook his fist at me.

Then his eyes rolled like marbles, he somersaulted like a five-year-old child and began to crawl on all fours.

Once he had gotten back up on his feet he began once again to laugh insanely:

"Why should a mad-doctor not go mad sometime? All you need to do is remember that the madness is temporary. A lung specialist can contract a lung illness and a urologist can fall victim to gonorrhea. Laughable. Age does not shield you from foolishness nor does life from death. Little tease," he tickled me under my chin.

"Goochie goochie goo—little murderer...."

I was ready to submit myself to the verdict of any court of law.

The court convened straight away.

The trial took place in the institution's church.

God the Father presided.

He sat before the altar with a pointed, star-studded cotton-candy cone on his head, and had put on horn-rimmed glasses in order to lend himself an air of authority. Above him, in a cage that was connected by a system of rods to a pillar, floated the Holy Ghost: the dove, who occasionally interrupted the holy procedure with inappropriate laughter.

The members of the committee in a half-circle around God the Father: God the Son, Munk's son, the beautiful boy; the Exorcist, the theosoph; the dancer; the general; the aristocratic gentleman; the Hasidic rabbi; the old newlyweds.

"Darling," whispered the toothless lips.

"My sweet," echoed the old man.

At first the Exorcist wanted to take on the defense. But I was sufficient for my own defense. There could be no absolution, only the administration of justice.

The prosecution was represented by the Albino who spoke down from the pulpit. He could find no severe word that I had not formulated more aggressively, no argument against me that I myself had not more logically and trenchantly expressed. The stream of his speech lapped into monotone.

Only on occasion did it swell into cascades and waterfalls and then I began to listen with interest.

I sat at the prayer bench before the altar.

The sun played through the stained-glass windows, through the glass bodies of the saints. The first nice day in weeks.

And again the Albino raised his voice:

"And so I move against the defendant on the grounds of the simulation of a non-existent physical and spiritual state—I also hold that his so-called hemorrhage was but a vulgar ruse, an attempt to escape his earthly judges, in order to find refuge and protection in our district—on the grounds of the assumption of a false name, blasphemy committed through the adoration of the heathen God Yenkadi, seduction of a minor (the case of Marianne) as well as two counts of murder: of his wife Maria and of the Detective Eva Zumbusch, aka Hyacinth: and I move for a double death-sentence at the executioner's axe, eternal damnation, the payment of alimony (the case of Marianne), and the revocation of his civil rights."

God the Father nodded in approval.

The dove laughed.

The son shone.

The Hasidic rabbi davened.

The Exorcist wore a distressed frown—the beautiful boy had a tear in his eye.

I stood up from the bench.

XXXIII

THE CONFESSION

IF, gentlemen of the jury, I may here lay down an open word and a candid confession, clarify the psychological bases of my guilt and fate, and strive to disentangle some threads knotted by God or the Devil, this will not be done to beg you for mercy or clemency. Mercy and clemency are not due to me. Quite the contrary, I would like to request your incorruptible and unforgiving judgment. I demand justice: for myself and for society and for the human community whom I have desecrated and thrown into fear and misery. I demand justice, and when you have weighed all that is in my favor and all that is against me—though in truth there is only that which is against me—you will render a judgment, which can only ring out thus: guilty, guilty, and thrice guilty.

Perhaps everything would have ended differently, perhaps my life would have passed in peace and blessedness—Spinoza says that blessedness is not the reward of virtue, but that virtue is in fact blessedness itself—had, opposite the house of my parents, the house with the two donkey heads, a meat market and butchery not been established, and had I not through ridiculous coincidence become acquainted with the butcher's son, a boy by the name of Munk, at an age considered to be the most sensitive and susceptible. Munk and I became friends and blood brothers and I went, after being summoned by Munk and out of childish curiosity alone, for the first time into the butcher's shop, where I palpated the dead and gutted calves and pigs. In the court-yard I was more astounded than frightened as I observed a gigantic ox collapsing under the butcher's hammer. But then, as if in a game, I dipped my finger in warm blood and licked it off. And then it was all over for me. That same day I came across a little butcher's knife shining in the sun. It lay on a windowsill, still bloodstained, where it might have been left by a negligent butcher's boy. Still, I hesitated. My temples thundered behind my forehead. My heart was in my throat. Although I was barely 13, I felt—no, I knew that the most important decision of my life stood before me. A whirl of sun leapt around the knife like a hellebore. I looked around shyly in case someone was nearby. Then I made a grab for the knife and hid it in my jacket.

My misdeeds began when I used this knife to inflict minor wounds on a tame bunny rabbit that I had at home and which I loved very much. The poor animal's convulsions delighted me and filled me with even more intimate affection for the tender creature. Often its pain would move me to tears. Then I kissed the wounds that raised purple-red from its white fur and drank its fresh, hot blood. And one day I could no longer withstand my desire.

It was a Sunday afternoon. My mother and father were out. I had remained at home feigning a headache. I squinted sluggishly in the sun—my misdeeds were all accompanied by beautiful weather and the sun always shone; I find it ridiculous and utterly incongruous to reality how sensationalist scribblers set the crimes of their vacuous horror novels at midnight or in a thunderstorm with romantic scenery. The sun shines over the righteous and the wicked. Anyway, I squinted in the sun until my eye turned red and then—again I saw the knife shining in the sun. I gripped the knife, slunk into the rabbit hutch in the courtyard, pulled the bunny rabbit out by both its long ears—it still had leaves of cabbage in its panting mouth—and while the tears were already flowing and my love almost cried out, my conscience winding and bending in anticipated remorse, I stabbed the bunny rabbit in the neck with the knife. A stream of blood arched out which I tried to catch with my mouth. And I drank and drank the red blood till I was drunk and, half unconscious, sank behind a rain barrel in a corner of the courtyard.

The evening dew awakened and sobered me. I awoke with a disgusting taste in my mouth. I wiped my brow. I was disgusted with myself. What had just happened? Then I saw the dead bunny rabbit lying next to me and the bloodstained knife. And at once I knew everything. Sobbing, I threw myself over the little animal's corpse. I hugged and kissed it as if it were a child. Then, furtively, I carried it into the vegetable garden and dug a grave in the potato patch with my bare hands. I stuck the knife above the grave as a cross and swore to never again commit murder. With gummy red eyes I went up into the house. My parents had still not returned. I undressed, lay down in bed and collapsed into a fiery fever that lasted weeks.

Once I had recovered I believed myself to have also been cured of my criminal insanity. I looked openly and freely into the sun—there was no knife to shine in it. I never entered the butchery again, as much as my friend Munk (Munk my enemy) tried to tempt me to do so. I studied diligently at school, became that which one calls a good student and left grammar school as primus omnium, furnished with a prize in "Antique Heroics." I studied law without passion for any particular vocation and my life was totally bereft of the extraordinary. I was active in the Teutonia fraternity and led a normal existence: study, dueling, some relationships, morning and early evening drinks, a little theatre on the weekends. I crossed swords with my opponent and could not suppress a certain feeling of wellbeing when I saw the blood run down his face. Already my poetical, satirical and musical talents began to manifest at the bar in all sorts of lewd songs and couplets which I presented at festive occasions, foundation anniversaries, commercia and so on to general applause, accompanying myself on the piano. I became a clerk, a J.D., became inactive at Teutonia, advanced to assessor.

Then one day on a compulsory visit to a counselor I made the acquaintance of his seventeen-year-old daughter, a thin, blonde, blue-eyed creature possessing extraordinary physical and spiritual charms. I had barely looked into these blue eyes when I knew that destiny stood before me for a second time.

I was gripped by an unspeakable passion for this beautiful girl and she rejected my love. But I was persistent and before a year had passed we were a couple. Our blessedness knew no bounds. We inhabited a little house all our own. I was made a partner of my father-in-law's firm. The work was not excessively strenuous—we could enjoy our young love from the ground up.

Then one day I noticed that my wife occasionally went red and white in turn and that she (it was summer) would cough into her handkerchief.

I was very worried, wanted to send for the doctor, but she only laughed at me.

One morning I discovered a handkerchief that she had cast aside: little red ringed flecks of blood.

I clutched my heart.

First black then red shone before my eyes.

I pressed the handkerchief to my lips and kissed the drops of blood.

There was no doubt—my wife suffered from a pulmonary hemorrhage. I loved—and today still love—my wife more than anything in the world. I wrapped her in my arms with devout tenderness and this tenderness was neither feigned nor simulated. I suggested to her that she should consult the doctor, but she laughed at me—over such trifles?—this will pass—and at heart, in my subconscious this answer gladdened me. A part of me did not want the doctor to come. A horrifying thought had taken possession of me that would not release me from its polypped arms. In secret I desired that Maria—such was the name of my wife—would bleed out in my arms, that she should, as once did Christ for the believers, give her blood for my sake. And I desired to drink her blood as Eucharist. It seemed to me that this alone could be the final realization of both her and my life. And thus I became a vampire, a murderer for love, a murderer without the act.

In the weeks that followed I loved her ever more frantically, ever more ecstatically.

"Most beloved," she occasionally smiled, her eyes like damp blue blooms of gentian, "I am so happy that this happiness cannot last. I feel I must die—and I die willingly."

So my morbid intoxication had already penetrated her subconscious. She wanted to die—just as I did.

I knew, that is to say my conscious mind did not know, but my subconscious knew, that in her physical condition my ardent, sensual love would have to kill her, that her tender nymphic body could not bear my vaultings—and yet I loved her ever wilder, and ever more blessedly did she give herself to me.

And one day it happened.

In the middle of our embrace blood burst from her mouth in a hot stream. The blood flowed over my naked body and I drank her heart's blood from her lips. My lips were stuck to hers, glued together with blood.

As the intoxication ebbed into blessed tiredness, I felt Maria's lips growing cold, I ripped my lips free, I saw in horror her wide open eyes: I held a corpse in my arms.

I had murdered Maria with my love.

The doctor determined the cause of death to be suffocation through hemorrhage.

I knew better.

I collapsed, as once after the death of the bunny rabbit, into a fiery fever; when the funeral took place I lay in half-delirium and heard only the bells droning into my twilight.

After some weeks I came to.

The doctor diagnosed the same illness in me as was in my wife: consumption.

I went abroad to convalesce.

I gave up my profession and allowed myself at first to be supported by my step-parents. And I remembered my bar-tried skills, finished contemporary couplets and reaped gold and laurels. During the war I sang war songs, and revolutionary songs during the revolution. I turned like a weathercock with the wind. From this I made a name for myself. Many names. A critic once compared me very flatteringly to Bellman, the great Swedish singer. And I was kept by all sorts of men and women and I dirtied and disgraced Maria's memory. I received anonymous letters addressed "to the pimp"—and the sender was not so wrong. But no one knew that the crimes I had committed were much worse, that my conscience was weighted down by centners, that I had murdered the one dearest to me in the whole world, and that the true address would have read:

"To the murderer..."

And now, gentlemen of the jury, give your verdict. I await your sentence with baited breath—as well as the day when in the red of morning my head will roll in the sawdust. My open eyes will watch, lusting for the blood spurting from the stump of my neck—

XXXIV

THE JUDGMENT

SUCH was my speech.

The jury retired for deliberation.

After just a quarter of an hour, God the Father in his capacity as foreman of the jury pronounced:

"Not guilty!"

He had opened the Bible, adjusted his horn-rimmed glasses and read in monotone:

"Book of Numbers Chapter 35 Verse 25: And the congregation shall deliver the slayer out of the hand of the revenger of blood."

I collapsed on the bench as though smote by thunder, struck by lightning.

Not guilty? Me?

"Godless God!" I cried, "bribed wretches, bribed by my bribing dialectic, perjurers of your juror's oath, bought and sold in the face of an open plea of guilt—who commanded you so shamelessly to bend the law? I am a murderer and demand my rights. It's your duty to deliver them to me. I insist on being condemned and put to death."

I began to froth at the mouth. But God the Father smiled mildly. He closed the bible with a clap, folded his glasses and he looked at me with his shining, beautiful eyes:

"Self likes sin
Self's a blight.
Self shuns sin
Self's alright.
Self is glass or clay
Self is love or hate
Self is plate or plater
Self is killer or creator
Self is pure and dull as gall
Self is alone yet all.
Self is good
Self is wicked
Self is blood
Self is giblets
Self alone can live itself
Self alone can lift itself
Self alone discerns itself
Self alone will burn itself
Be at peace ye good and depraved
Self alone can save itself!"

The beautiful boy collapsed over his cross, weeping.

"So I sacrificed myself for humanity for nothing!"

God the Father spoke:

"To this one," and he indicated me, "you were of no use, this one lay outside your power and strength—you've done enough for yourself..."

I was led away screaming and gesticulating; the Exorcist gave me his hand in farewell, the Albino clapped me on the back: "What did I always say—you are an innocent little lamb. All the best and hopefully we will never meet again—I hope that for you. Do greet the outside world for me."

Against my will I was shown the door and given my freedom.

XXXV

THE FIRST STEPS

THEN I stood alone in the monstrous expanse and had no idea where to begin with my existence. The expanse vaulted over me like a cupola of Michaelangelo, gigantic in dimensions, strict in its laws which were consummate but finite. A giant would grind its head against the vault of heaven.

Eternal time, eternity, exists to such a tiny extent as eternal space, infinity, I thought. We live in a universe that encompasses 999 million solar systems; in one of these systems we play our abject rolls: hammy actors dressed up like kings and prophets in golden frippery and colorful scraps. If we bend our nose over the microscope and observe drops of water: there infusoria and rotifers march the same elliptical orbit as the stars in space. And every crumb of soil exhibits the same reciprocal motion. The protoplast wanders tirelessly with kernel and grain. A person wanders like a star, infusorium and protoplast and each human cell whirls in its own orbit on the same miraculous course. A soul wanders in the same way: and glances from a star onto this crumb of earth and gets dizzy. Then it looks from an infusorium stuck in this crumb of earth up to the people above and it gets seasick.

I was again betrayed to the wild world, helpless and defenseless.

There were no longer any walls to protect me. No little window to dim the light and to dull and filter it before it reaches my sick eyes.

The sun burned unbearably. At any minute I'd have to shut my eyes.

I turned back and rung the bell at the institution's portal.

The head of the white-haired doorman with his old, tattered soldier's cap darted like a fantastic serpent's head out of the little window.

"What do you want?"

I kneeled:

"Please take me back into my cell—which protects me—from the world—from myself."

The doorman sneered:

"Are you crazy? You've been released. The madhouses, hospitals and prisons are overflowing. We have no need for superfluous, redundant boarders." His mouth became broad like the mouth of an ox. "Steal a bicycle or kill someone and then come back!"

The window clanged shut.

I staggered through the streets.

The people stole glances at me as I groped my way along the houses, too scared to cross an empty space.

Some shop-girls came out of their shops and laughed. But then they met my gaze and were frightened.

What should I have done? What should I have thought? I didn't know.

Dusk rose like a gray mist from the pavement.

I landed in a public park.

I searched for the darkest bench and sat down.

I don't know how long I'd been sitting there when a tender voice asked me:

"Do you want to love me?"

I looked up and saw the silhouette of a girl.

I couldn't make out her face or her age.

"I can't love anymore, girl. I've loved too much."

"Oh," she laughed softly, "if it's just that."

She touched me playfully.

Then she put herself gently on top of me, moving up and down, and loved me as if I were a woman and she were a man. I let it happen in silence.

A little passive, physiological happiness—what more? Did I still have a will to happiness?

She sat down next to me and brought her face close to mine:

"Now do you believe you can love?"

I was silent.

"Why don't you say anything?"

She saw that my head was buzzed.

"Where did you come from?"

I was silent.

"Oh, I know where you came from. You came from the grey house. Is that right?"

I was silent.

"You don't need to answer me. I know it for sure. The people who sit in this park on the darkest benches are always the ones who were just released from the grey house a couple streets over. They still don't know what to do with themselves. They look for darkness. But I'm gonna show you a star in the darkness. The star of hope."

I found all this overly sentimental and stayed silent.

She paused for a bit, then:

"Are you a pimp? Do you wanna be mine? I need a strong guy. And you didn't go soft in the grey house."

She tested my muscles.

I broke my silence.

"I'm a murderer."

I felt her hesitate.

Then she whistled softly through her teeth.

"Ooh la la! I never would have guessed. Yup, then I have nothing but respect for you. I was once engaged to a murderer named Munk. And I also had his kid. His name's Christian and he's the most beautiful person you can imagine. He's seventeen now and a little crazy, unfortunately. How long were you in the spa for?"

"A year."

"Manslaughter with mitigating circumstances?"

"No."

She hesitated again.

"So you bid adieu to Father Phillip without asking him?"

"No—I was absolved."

She laughed.

"Boy oh boy you're lucky. We should celebrate. Do you have any money?"

I shook my head.

"No worries. I still have a bit of cash. Wanna go for a drink at the 'Blue Ape'?"

XXXVI

THE BLUE APE
AND THE GREEN BIRD

THE blue ape was a basement joint, I no longer know on which street.

She had linked arms with me and it was clear that she was proud of me, that she was showing me off.

An absolved murderer for a lover—that's no small thing.

She whispered with the guy behind the bar who was as big and fat as a hippopotamus with tiger paws.

The men and women sitting in the joint all examined me with sideways glances.

All the men looked like me and all the girls looked like the one who had hooked up with me.

"Well done!"

The bartender came over and shook my hand. He whispered with the guests. They were mostly fences who concealed their stolen wares under their coats: shawls and shoes that hung by their laces around their necks.

And ceremoniously they all walked past me in a long row and shook my hand.

One of the last of them introduced himself politely:

"Sally Koffertraeger, but my friends call me Snail."

The introduction was so dignified, he spoke his name so articulately, that I was now obligated to have a friendly conversation with him, which seemed to his liking. Maybe he'd never gone so far as murder. Maybe he thought we could team up sometime.

"Hey, how's it going?" I asked.

He shrugged his shoulders:

"Did you read today's paper?"

I said I hadn't.

He took a sheet out of his pocket and showed me a headline:

FABULOUS BREAK-IN
TWO STORIES UP WITH DRILLS
AND TORCHES

"Yes—and?"

He tapped his chest, which was hidden beneath a green woolen sweater:

"That was us!"

He puffed up like a turkey.

"And how'd it turn out?"

He lowered his voice:

"Between me and you, we just broke even. Three hundred marks in the safe. A hundred each: there were three of us. Rotten luck, no? In a rage I took the green bird that was sitting on a perch in the room where the safe was standing."

I hesitated:

"What sort of green bird?"

He pointed backwards:

"I gave him to the bartender."

On the cigar boxes behind the bar sat Lora, my parrot.

Sally Koffertraeger, a.k.a. Snail, had broken into my old apartment.

I was too far gone to begrudge him that.

The collosal technical effort with the drills and the torches hadn't really paid off.

After approaching the parrot and petting his head he recognized me; he rolled his eyes so that only the orange-yellow in them was visible and squawked: "Come *iiin*. Come my doll. Come on in. Pet my little head."

174

The bird's voice had lost all its horror.

He seemed to have forgotten the name Maria after not hearing it for so long.

The girl laughed.

The bartender slapped his stomach.

I had to laugh. But a tear hung on my eyelashes.

"Maria!" I said to the bird to jog its memory.

It looked at me sideways, rolled its eyes and said nothing.

XXXVII

THE HOUSE IN THE ABYSS

"I have nowhere to stay."

"I'll take care of that."

The girl wrapped herself in her shawl.

I followed her.

We crisscrossed our way through a number of streets.

"NO" was written on some street sign.

We ducked into a dark hallway.

The door to the house stood open. The door to a courtyard.

We crossed three courtyards.

At the third building back we stumbled into a basement. The girl opened the unlocked door. Then she took me by the hand.

"Careful! Don't wake anyone! They're lying on the floor everywhere like corpses. You've gotta place your feet like a dancer."

A terrible stench filled the hole.

We strode through two chambers.

The girl came to a stop in the third.

"This is where I stay."

She began to undress.

I did the same.

Soon I felt her little girlish breasts in my hands.

And we sank dully onto the straw in a corner.

It must have already been morning for a while, but the chamber was still filled with a barely-penetrable twilight.

Above us dirty light filtered through narrow cracks.

This must have been a sort of window. I eventually discerned that the apparent windows were covered with brown paper—probably so that no one could see in from the courtyard.

I stayed with the girl for eight days.

Both antechambers swarmed with rats and children. In one corner lay an older man blind from white lead poisoning. A one-year-old child sat on his stomach and played with his red beard. A syphilitic whore decayed in another corner. She had cards laid out in front of her. She played with the jack and king of hearts and said "sweety!" to them; when she noticed me she told my fortune from the cards: "An engagement is in store. A letter is on its way. Beware a black-haired person. A long journey is in sight."

The children never saw light or had fresh air. They had no shirts, no pants, no clothes. Only rags hung off them. They had never made it out of the courtyard and had to tell fairy tales that began: "Once upon a time there was a child who had a snow-white shirt and enough bread to be full every day..."

"Once upon a time there was a star that spread light and mild warmth over the earth, and all the people who walked in its rays shone gold and silver, and this star was called the sun...."

"Once upon a time there was a forest with a vast host of trees like the one that stands in the courtyard but thousands upon thousands all together..."

"Once upon a time there was a bird that looked like a sparrow, grey and unsightly, but it didn't squawk like a rusted door hinge: it sang like an angel from heaven. This bird was called the nightingale..."

The children gaped with their inflamed eyes and opened their scabbed lips wide.

And the oldest spoke:

"None of what you're telling's true. But the stories are good. Keep going…"

Lying in the dark on the straw and the lice and insects were crawling all over me, now and then a rat jumping over my leg, I thought of the fate of these children.

And I couldn't understand why their parents didn't gather them in all their nakedness into a terrifying parade of thousands and march them, silent and wild, through the streets of the rich: and at their head with a wooden cross on his back, Christian, the beautiful boy and son of Maria, who had her sleeping chamber in the third dugout: Christian, who thought himself God's Son, and who was in fact the insane son of a whore and a murderer. He had in truth chosen the best profession for himself because no other profession was open to these children of the abyssal house besides thief, pimp, fencer, robber and murderer.

XXXVIII

THE CHINESE WOMAN

ONE evening when I didn't know where to begin with myself and the world, I found strange and colorful paper slips and lanterns hanging in front of a bar near Am Kroegel. I came nearer, saw a pale girl (on one of these paper slips) who was gazing tenderly up at a terrifying warrior. And between the two ran a script that was indecipherable to me. It all had something to do with an advertising for a Chinese juggling or theater troupe. I entered through a narrow, damp passage. It opened into a hall: and upon a primitive stage with no scenery I saw the same play that I had seen on the poster: a pale girl kneeled down tenderly before a terrifying warrior who was brandishing a sword. In that moment she stood up, pattered up to the forestage, and it almost seemed that she was speaking directly to me what she then whispered and chirped and smiled in an incomprehensible idiom to the audience. And although I didn't know her language, I understood everything; she wanted to make clear to me that she loves that terrifying man with the sword, her executioner who must kill her under orders from the Mandarin, but that she dies willingly by his hand and that she will eternally whir around his head as the bird by morning, as the butterfly by noon, as the bat by night. Then she pattered back, kneeled down, the executioner struck wordlessly—a shriek of horror from the audience, I fell white as chalk onto a column; the head rolled over the boards, blood sprayed over her, the curtain fell. It was all smoke and mirrors, of course. But I was so dazed that I went out onto the courtyard. I thought back to how I had once killed the bunny rabbit and Maria. Had I not been the executioner who swung his curved sword on that stage—not under orders from the Mandarin but under the orders of my own heart?

The little Chinese woman was standing at the stage's exit and looking at the moon that hung high in space. She looked so enchanting, so unearthly, as she turned her head wordlessly to me like an animal and observed me without thoughts or feelings. I came closer and directed a couple of words at her in English. She shook her head. I didn't know what to do—my heart was in my throat. I gripped her hand and, just as she had done before the executioner, I kneeled down before her. And I kissed this tender, delicate hand, softly.

A gong sounded inside. She slipped away. I was alone. I headed home.

I lay sleeplessly next to the girl in my room that smelled of tar and I saw the little Chinese woman in the darkness, how she kneelt down before her lover, the executioner. That was when I devised my first Chinese poem. It was quite short, that which the Japanese call *Hokku*:

> You love the executioner.
> He kills you every day.
> Your blood flows eternally.
> But you smile.

The next evening I returned to the spot. When I entered she was playing a little comedy: a student in love with the saleswoman of a perfume business. He cannot confess his love to her because a revoltingly ugly old woman, the keeper of the shop, is always present. Finally he is able to slip the girl—she was played by my little Chinese woman—a note: tonight at the temple there and there. She smiled her agreement. Second scene: in the temple. The student boozing with an old bonze. He awaits his girl. She doesn't come. The two boozers grow tired. They fall asleep arm in arm. Then the girl arrives with a little paper lantern. She bends over the two sleeping men. Her face makes no expression. She strips one of her slippers from her foot and lays it down in the student's lap. Disappears with her lantern like a firefly. The student awakens, rubs his eyes, finds the slipper and is inconsolable. Curtains. I went out onto the courtyard. The little Chinese woman stood there once again. I handed her a bouquet of mimosa that I had pilfered from the flower shop. She seemed to laugh. Then she took my hand for a second. When I came the next evening I no longer saw the colorful paper slips or the Chinese lanterns. In the hall where yesterday the handsome tale of the slipper had played out, clerks, workers, soldiers and wild women danced fervently.

I went to the innkeeper enthroned behind his bar. "Where are the Chinese?"

"They set off early this morning. By the way, are you the one who brought the bouquet of mimosa to the star of the ensemble yesterday?"

I said yes, my heart pounding.

"I have something for you."

He gave me a little package.

I opened it in a corner next to a glass Hellen. Inside were two tiny slippers and a note upon which was written: "Mai Lung Fang greets you. Mai Lung Fang dictated these words for a friend for you. Mai Lung Fang loves you as you love Mai Lung Fang. Mai Lung Fang loves art and those who love art. Peace and happiness be with you!"

I stumbled over to the bar.

"Do you know Mai Lung Fang's next address? Where she's going?"

The innkeeper knit his brow:

"Mai Lung Fang? Mai Lung Fang? That was the young Chinese guy who played the lovely girl roles? And deceptively well. A delightful boy! If you didn't know you wouldn't be able to tell him from a girl. Get this, there was once a young sailor here who fell madly in love with Mai Lung Fang because he thought she was a girl..."

He started to snort like a seal.

I felt a quiet twinge in my heart.

184

The weather had become horrible. The
rain clapped on the windows. And in the
rhythm of the rolling drops I formed my other Hokku:

> The rain runs.
> I loved a phantom.
> The clouds blow—
> Where blows my fate?

XXXIX

THE BOXING MATCH

DRIFTING through the streets like a leaf in the autumn wind, I was blown before a wall of posters in a corner. There I read in loud colors, black and white on red:

Sensational!
Today only! Boxing match
in the Great Theatre
at the Weidendammer Bridge!
The Title Fight for the World Championship
for World Domination
Between Munk, Master of Europe, a.k.a.
Dictator
Mundi, and the Asian Master Mai Lung Fang,
a.k.a. the Chinese Wildcat!
Do Not Miss this Decisive Moment
in World History.

I did not want to miss it and proceeded through a side door of the Great Theater into the dressing rooms where I met Munk, playing with his muscles, in the middle of a grand monologue that would've worked well just as well in the arena:

"I am stepping into the ring myself. No one can say that I'm a coward. In me the continent is embodied and sublimated. The great hour is upon us. The question is: Europe or Asia? The white or the yellow race? Schinderhannes and Schopenhauer, to name two opposite extremes—or Lao Tzu and Li Hung-chang? Schnapps or opium? To whom belongs the future that will be called eternity? My muscles are steeled. I have been trained. I have read Lao Tzu. I will strike the yellow man with his own weapon. No one has anything on me. For two months I have touched no woman. I am bursting with virility. Responsibility tones me. I already hear the champions of Gliwic, Nancy, Warsaw, Czernowitz, Malmo and Naples singing: *ave Caesar, morituri te salutant...*"

I stood next to the dressing room mirror in silence.

Munk took no notice of me.

The manager stumbled in excitedly.

Munk asked in a patronizing tone: "How goes it?"

The manager: "Great! I'm here to check your gloves and bandages."

Munk stuck out his leather-covered fists:

"Fist and blood and heart are one."

The manager beamed: "Victory seems clear."

"Seems?"

"Clear as crystal."

"What are they betting?"

"5:4"

"Too little. Do the people not love me anymore?"

Munk stomped his feet.

The manager placated him:

"They love you inexpressibly. But in boxing they judge one's qualities as a boxer."

"I've trained for two months."

"The Chinese knocked Carpentier the world champion out in seven minutes."

"I have emerged to avenge the white race."

"Europe heard it and shuddered, bewildered. No one's been pictured as much as you in the illustrateds. Now's the time to gather all your strength. No digression. Boxing is a matter of egocentric world-view. Here it's you or me. Not: you and me. You have to knock him out."

Christian, Munk's son, stumbled into the wardrobe.

"Father—I implore you—what are you doing—he'll crush you."

Munk looked in the mirror:

"Who's that little boy? Oh, my son—"

The manager grew nervous.

"Please don't mess this up. I bet a hundred thousand marks on you."

Munk:

"Don't worry, my darling, I have nerves like ship ropes. What do you want, son? You don't care about me for months then—"

Christian shook his blonde locks.

"I was thinking of you the whole time—"

"Pure sentiment. He who really thinks, acts."

"Your picture hangs over my bed, God knows."

"Ridiculous. A naked little whore would be more suitable."

"I love you."

"Yugh, I don't love you."

Christian lifted his hands piously:

"Let me enter the arena in your stead. The Chinese will kill you."

Munk bubbled up like seltzer water:

"Nonsense—here: feel one of my biceps."

Christian spoke, now more quietly:

"You are strong. But I am weak."

"An anemic little boy. I am strength, wildness and dignity. I confront. My juice boils. How I made you is a mystery to me. I had already had 12 Kulmbachers. And I didn't want you: you nothing, you barely, you oh…"

The boy smiled sadly:

"I am meekness. Meekness prevails. Pipe bends. Oaks fall. Clouds blow in the storm— towers crash."

Munk scowled:

"Symbols have no affect on me."

The boy grew more persistent:

You only have your life, your position. If you succumb then your power is at an end, your life is at an end. The people will laugh you all the way to Tehran. You want to rule. So stay. Ruling is your happiness. I sacrifice myself for you gladly. But it would not truly be a sacrifice: since I cannot succumb."

Munk aimed a punch at the ball that was hanging from the ceiling.

"Go to the zoo. Have the kangaroos teach you boxing. Then come back."

The manager interrupted him with a hoarse, excited voice: "The bell. Are you ready?"

Munk squared himself:

"I am."

He went past me and Christian with great steps without deigning to glance at us.

Deafening applause sounded from the arena.

Christian and I stood like caryatids to the left and right of the door.

We didn't say a word.

We knew the result of the fight all too well.

Mai Lung Fang had already defeated me. He could take on any form.

After maybe five minutes Munk was brought in on a stretcher, streaming blood.

The Chinese had knocked both eyes out of his head.

There was no longer a European world-view.

I heard the manager screeching:

"Thank God we have an institute for artificial human eyes in Berlin. Berlin at the forefront of Germany, Germany at the forefront of Europe, Europe at the forefront of the world."

I approached the stretcher.

"Do you recognize me, Munk."

Christian stroked him with confused hands.

I received no answer.

I slipped out of the house covertly and attracted no attention, just as I had come.

XXXX

THE BRACELET

I left the girl after eight days.

She gave me her hand, looked me in the eyes one last time and kissed me softly on the lips.

I went through the streets and again I didn't know where my path would lead. I was covered in lice from head to toe. But I'd already won that comradely relationship with lice of the poor and miserable, for whom bugs, lice, and rats are better brothers and sisters than human beings.

I strayed through the streets. A boy whispered in my ear: "You want to make your fortune?" I nodded. He took dirty receipts from his pocket on which numbers were scribbled with pencil. He spoke: "One lot costs five marks. It's father's lottery. There at the door.

Grand prize fifteen marks. Take a lot." I had no money to make my fortune.

I went aground in front of a bookstore display and looked to see if any of my books were out. I read: *Proper German for Military Hopefuls*; *The German Underworld in its Sociopolitcal, Literary, Linguistic Formation*; *Beginners Rotwelsch*; *The New Pitaval* was opened. I read the chapter heading: "The Confession." It was my confession. It was already in print.

I stood in front of brightly-lit shop windows and considered with interest the displays at the leather store and the jewelers.

I admired a suitcase. Real vulcanized fiber.

If I were to travel away? A knotted walking stick in a cane and umbrella display drew me to itinerancy.

What if I went wandering?

I wasn't too old to hoof it.

Dogs barked.

A cop oinked at me:

"If you could please make an effort not to stand in the middle of the causeway?"

A weird trinket in the display window of a jewelry store drew my gaze.

Attention! Sensation! Bargain!
Bracelet made of real human eyes!

I was distressed by a compulsion to find out the bracelet's price.

So the man with the cart managed to get rid of it. I entered the elegant store, shaggy and debauched though I was.

The manager gawked.

I stuttered:

"I would like to know the price of the bracelet made of human eyes on display."

The manager examined me from head to toe:

"If you could please leave the premises."

On the way out I heard:

"That thug is scheming to rob us."

I stood again before the display window.

"These eyes here," I sensed, "are Maria's, and these here are Hyacinth's."

I gave other eyes the names of other women I had loved. Munk's eyes, too, I saw among them. Only one pair of eyes was missing: Marianne's eyes.

I knew that somewhere she held watch for me through the dust of streets and stars, that she awaited me in a muffled, blessed calm and that two children's eyes followed her gaze into the darkness.

I heard a voice next to me:

"This is mischief! Treachery! The eyes in the bracelet aren't real human eyes—they are artificial. I see that right away. I am the proprietor of an institute for artificial human eyes."

I turned around and noticed a fat, stately little gentleman wearing a mink coat.

"Excuse me—"

The gentleman examined me with critical rigor.

"Excuse me," I continued, "I have witnessed so much want and misery, crime and madness on this earth that my eyes hurt and I often want to rip them from my head. Perhaps through your artificial eyes you see red and blue and gold and silver like on postcards. Could you manufacture a bespoke pair of artificial eyes for me?"

The fat gentleman looked at me with surprise.

"You should go and get disinfected before you speak to me."

This jab aroused cheer and suppressed laughter in a standing passerby.

"And for your information: a bespoke pair of artificial eyes costs five thousand marks. The first half of the sum is due upon ordering. There are all sorts of unreliable people..."

He winked which emboldened the audience that had gathered to chuckle and smirk.

I looked through the fat man as if he were glass. How strange—I had forgotten that you need money to live. The concept of "money"—I had forgotten it.

XXXXI

IN THE HOMELESS SHELTER

LATE in the evening, dead tired from running back and forth without goal or purpose, I entered the homeless asylum.

Looking in the washroom, a need for hygiene awakened in me with more than physical power. You have to go clear again, I thought, yes, you must: a clear, a clean, a cleanly person.

I linked up with the convoy streaming into the washroom. I undressed. In the meantime my clothes were deloused in a gigantic steaming kettle.

Then I stood for a quarter of an hour under the cold shower. Oh, that did me good.

At the entrance to the dormitory I received a thin blanket and a bowl for food. There was an atmosphere of thick, sticky warmth: as it had been when I walked through the fantastic forest. Oh! How long ago that was! Strain as I might, I could no longer recall.

I lay at the wall of the women's ward.

A nailed door separated it from the men's ward.

Secret knocks both ways.

"Comrade," said someone next to me who was sewing his shirt in the dim light, "wait for night. Then we break the door in. There are lovely women lying over there."

Someone played the harmonica.

> "Early in the morning
> when the hens do crow—"

Some sang along.

There was noise from the women's section.

The harmonica went silent.

It sounded through the wall, clear and distinct:

> Such a pretty thing was I
> Always smart and lithe
> Then one came down from Borsig
> the dough, the brains on this guy!
> No one as darling as he was
> with his little red tie.
> He bought me a brand new hat.

Who knows why love's like that.
O Berlin, how fine
is your realm divine.
In our hometown
lovely girls abound.
Swim over. Tralala.

I always had him here.
But then he disappeared.
I was eight months along on
A windy night that shook with storm
I shlepped up on the common
and buried the poor worm.
My blood boiled, I cursed and I spat.
Who knows why love's like that.
O Berlin, how fine
is your realm divine.
In our hometown
lovely girls abound.
Swim over. Tralala.

And now I'm turning tricks
I pay my mack and hustle dicks.
Then one night a wagon
the time I cannot say
started me a-draggin'
Into the Charité
There'r fleas in my blood, my heart is
    a gnat

Who knows why love's like that.
O Berlin, how fine
is your realm divine.
In our hometown
lovely girls abound.

Swim over. Tralala.
I'm sick without a prayer
But I don't really care.
The shepherd he herds sheep,
Here comes a friendly lad
I give him what to keep
think on me and please be glad.
Mercury and owl's fat,
Who knows why love's like that.
O Berlin, how fine
is your realm divine.
In our hometown
lovely girls abound.
Swim over. Tralala.

It became dark and quiet, over here and over there.

Wheezing, breathing, coughing, snoring, sighing.

"Hey you," someone jabbed me ineptly in the darkness. "Comrade, help, we're breaking down the door to the women's ward…"

We braced ourselves.

One guy commanded us like we were driving stakes or laying pavement, but very quietly:

"*Eins—hupp—Eins—hupp—*"

The door buckled.

The men scurried over like insects and soon each had a woman in his arm.

I crept slowly and felt for the encampment of the woman that was on the wall just opposite to mine.

And as I'm bending down, bringing my face close to the peaceful, deeply-sleeping woman who had a child in her arm, I realize that it's Marianne, whom I'd been seeking all these days with my desire and with my heart as a compass: Marianne, my girl, and our child.

And I held watch in silence like a cherub in front of her camp.

XXXXII

THE ROAD TO FREEDOM

THE next morning I awaited Marianne at the exit of the women's ward.

Sparrows and children danced in the sun, it had become spring over night and somewhere—miracle of the metropolis—there sang a nightingale.

Marianne skipped along beside me, she counted the cobblestones and played the primeval game of hop-scotch.

In my arm I carried the child, who grabbed at the sun with both hands.

I could and would find work, that was for certain. Life had to be followed through on. Oh, now it was beginning for the very first time: in the eyes of this beautiful girl, of this serene child; never before had such a life been lived: rapture of love, fanfare of duty, heaven of a thousand hells. It will begin with this spring day. A new global epoch will date from this day forward. The first year has begun. My lungs expanded: freedom! No more looking back! The chains were sprung. The sun still shone, my lungs still breathed, my heart still sung: like a nightingale.

To make money for today I established myself as a frantic luggage carrier at the Anhalter Bahnhof. I earned fifty marks.

That evening after having already eaten in a small inn, and having just crossed the bridge near the Reichstagufer on our way to cheap lodging in the north, we came across a man lying under a lantern.

At first I thought he was drunk.

I gave Marianne the child, drew near and shuddered back.

I thought I saw my own face, like in a mirror.

The man who lay there was dead. And the dead bear a striking resemblance to me.

Then a wild joy, a mystical plan flashed through me.

The dead man was elegant and could pass for me in earlier, now discarded times.

I groped in his breast pocket, opened his wallet: it contained a passport with the name Andreas Z....., born 1891, without occupation. I took the passport for myself and stuck the certificate of citizenship that had up till now legitimated me into the dead man's pocket.

So from then on my name was Andreas Z..... and my first self had died and here began my second, other self.

The child in my left arm, my right arm on Marianne's shoulders, over which her long blond braids rolled down so she looked like a schoolgirl, I went the next morning, in the first red of a balmy spring day, into the Schlesischer Bahnhof.

From Yenkadi's ashes I rose like a phoenix in new flight.

The morning post brought the news that Doctor X....., known to broader circles as an original composer of couplets and also for his guest appearances on stage, who had recently suffered from a severe hemorrhage, was found dead the previous night at the bridge on Reichstagufer.

Since the deceased had not been robbed and there was no sign of a violent death, a stroke was presumed. The press made note of his unexpected passing with lively regret.

I carry my fate in my hands before me. These eyes burn inwards and this heart beats under my skin. Because this forehead is so smooth the brain within it is all the more wrinkled, and this clear eye was bought with dark pain. Many unseen tears washed it clear. If you were to look closely you would find some white among my blonde hair. The traces of my time in prison, the hospital, and the madhouse have blown and washed away in the sand like foxes' steps in distant pine forests.

I sweep away wind and clouds and the world before my eyelashes when I so desire. Who can look at my stomach and see that it's been torn by hunger?

I stand at the threshold of my thirtieth year and as I look and listen back, there rushes and races a brown stream with white combs of spray: like the Inn or Bober at high water. And I look inside myself: and there's the same stream, but it is illuminated by strange lights that have flown here from far away like exotic fireflies. And I strain to hear forwards: there is the same noise. But I stride above the waters as once Christ over the Sea of Galilee. I dance, I skip, I jump. I fall to my knee, but I jump

back up to my feet: and stride. And below
rushes the stream over which I was supposed
to drive the souls of Maria and Marianne. I
hear Charon stalking and cursing. His ferry
is empty. The stream carries me like a *trottoir
roulant*.

A PARTIAL LIST OF SNUGGLY BOOKS

G. ALBERT AURIER *Elsewhere and Other Stories*
CHARLES BARBARA *My Lunatic Asylum*
S. HEZOLNRY BERTHOUD *Misanthropic Tales*
LÉON BLOY *The Tarantulas' Parlor and Other Unkind Tales*
ÉLÉMIR BOURGES *The Twilight of the Gods*
CYRIEL BUYSSE *The Aunts*
JAMES CHAMPAGNE *Harlem Smoke*
FÉLICIEN CHAMPSAUR *The Latin Orgy*
BRENDAN CONNELL *Metrophilias*
BRENDAN CONNELL *Unofficial History of Pi Wei*
BRENDAN CONNELL (editor)
    The Zinzolin Book of Occult fiction
RAFAELA CONTRERAS *The Turquoise Ring and Other Stories*
DANIEL CORRICK (editor)
    Ghosts and Robbers: An Anthology of German Gothic Fiction
ADOLFO COUVE *When I Think of My Missing Head*
QUENTIN S. CRISP *Aiaigasa*
LUCIE DELARUE-MARDRUS *The Last Siren and Other Stories*
LADY DILKE *The Outcast Spirit and Other Stories*
CATHERINE DOUSTEYSSIER-KHOZE
    The Beauty of the Death Cap
ÉDOUARD DUJARDIN *Hauntings*
BERIT ELLINGSEN *Now We Can See the Moon*
ERCKMANN-CHATRIAN *A Malediction*
ALPHONSE ESQUIROS *The Enchanted Castle*
ENRIQUE GÓMEZ CARRILLO *Sentimental Stories*
DELPHI FABRICE *Flowers of Ether*
DELPHI FABRICE *The Red Sorcerer*
DELPHI FABRICE *The Red Spider*
BENJAMIN GASTINEAU *The Reign of Satan*
EDMOND AND JULES DE GONCOURT *Manette Salomon*
REMY DE GOURMONT *From a Faraway Land*
REMY DE GOURMONT *Morose Vignettes*
GUIDO GOZZANO *Alcina and Other Stories*
GUSTAVE GUICHES *The Modesty of Sodom*
EDWARD HERON-ALLEN *The Complete Shorter Fiction*
EDWARD HERON-ALLEN *Three Ghost-Written Novels*